SIR PEREGRINE'S HEIR.

CHAPTER I.

COMING HOME.

"He is late. It is nearly six—the letter said five!" And the speaker, who was a pretty girl of some two-and-twenty years of age, glanced up at the huge clock of parcel-gilt bronze that stood conspicuous on the massive mantelpiece. It was ugly, although of French manufacture; that clock being one of those monumental monstrosities, in the taste of the First Empire, that English visitors to Paris bought so eagerly when the Peace permitted them to cross the channel. The very pedestal of black

marble might have done duty for a miniature mausoleum, and the dial-plate was
upheld by a grim figure of Time, with
scythe and hour-glass, sturdily mowing an
imaginary crop of human lives as the hours
went by. But it suited well with its surroundings at Crag Towers, and had never
been removed from the place of honour to
which the Lady Conyers of the period had
promoted it in the year of grace 1814.

" You need not be so impatient, sister
Nellie," answered a richer and a firmer voice;
" we are likely to have quite enough of
our nephew's society, and I, for one, am in
no hurry to see the underbred urchin,
whose father was never forgiven, yet who
is, it seems, to be owner one day of the
great Conyers' property, and representative
of the proud old Conyers' name."

She who had spoken last was the elder
by several years of the sisters, and presented as strong a contrast to her junior
as if there had been between them no
such close tie of relationship as actually

John Berwick Harwood

Sir Peregrine's Heir

Vol. 1

John Berwick Harwood

Sir Peregrine's Heir

Vol. 1

Reprint of the original, first published in 1875.

1st Edition 2024 | ISBN: 978-3-38525-140-3

Verlag (Publisher): Outlook Verlag GmbH, Zeilweg 44, 60439 Frankfurt, Deutschland
Vertretungsberechtigt (Authorized to represent): E. Roepke, Zeilweg 44, 60439 Frankfurt, Deutschland
Druck (Print): Books on Demand GmbH, In de Tarpen 42, 22848 Norderstedt, Deutschland

SIR PEREGRINE'S HEIR.

BY

JOHN BERWICK HARWOOD,

AUTHOR OF "LADY FLAVIA."

IN THREE VOLUMES.

VOL. I.

LONDON:

RICHARD BENTLEY AND SON,

NEW BURLINGTON STREET.

1875.

CONTENTS OF VOL. I.

existed. Nellie, the younger, was small, slight, and dark-eyed, with jet black hair that gleamed in the light of the sloping sun. Hers was a sweet, dainty little face, delicate as to features and pure as to complexion, and would have won even more admiration than it did, had not her gentle prettiness been flashed down, as it were, by the dazzling beauty of her elder sister.

Adeline Conyers, tall, fair, and stately, was one of those rare women who extort homage by the force of their overpowering loveliness. With her, face and figure seemed alike faultless, unless a captious critic had demurred to the unusual length of the white and slender throat on which the haughty head was poised so royally. Her hair was of that flaxen hue seldom seen but in Scandinavia, and which gave no reflex of gold in any light; and she wore it high on her head, in a feathery cloud, arranged with that exquisite art that counterfeits artlessness. Her eyes were large, and light grey in colour, while the slender length of her neck, of which mention has been made, had gained her the appellation of Swan-neck, similar to that borne so many centuries before by Edith, the discarded consort of our English Harold. Her singular beauty was, however, rendered less attractive, owing to the expression of innate pride which brooded upon the clear-cut lips and betrayed itself in the very glitter of the cold eyes. Her dress was of richer materials and more elaborate make than that of her younger sister, and the easy grace of manner that was an instinct with both had in her been rendered perhaps slightly artificial by early contact with foreign society. Miss Conyers had indeed been educated in Paris, where she had spent some years under the care of her uncle's widow, Mrs. Craven Conyers, who had long been domiciled in the aristocratic Faubourg St. Germain. It may be, perhaps, that these experiences had enhanced the natural arrogance of her temperament, but it is certain that she habitually regarded her home-staying younger sister with an air of lofty superiority.

"Remember, Adeline, he is our brother's child—poor Edmund's son," said Nellie timidly; but her imperious sister did not allow the sentence to be completed.

"The son of the brother who disgraced us all, and whose conduct embittered my father's life," she broke out angrily, pressing her small foot the firmer, as she spoke, upon the silken footstool on which it rested; "whose name, had justice been done, should have been struck out alike from the pedigree and the succession. I, for one, should have regarded the act as the mere lopping of a withered branch from the parent tree."

"That would have been a harsh punishment, I think," returned Nellie, mildly, "for poor Edmund's offence against the grandeur of our family. Beyond the one fact that he married some one of lower rank than his own, and of whom papa consequently did not approve, I never clearly understood what he had done;

but then you know, Adeline, I was so young when he went away that I do not remember him in the least."

"I can recollect him," answered the elder sister, compressing her lips, "though I, too, was but a child when he left Crag Towers for the last time. He was good-looking and good-humoured, and meant, I am sure, to be a kind brother, but there was nothing of the Conyers in his nature, and his chosen friends were people from whom he picked up what are called modern ideas. Papa, I know, was often hurt and angry at the opinions he would utter here before half the county. And then he put the seal to his disobedience by marrying the daughter of a north-country farmer. I shall never forget the voice in which my father bade me consider him as dead, and to mention his name no more."

"I think Edmund's regiment was under orders to return from India to England, when he fell ill and died?" said Nellie, interrogatively.

"Yes," answered her sister, "he had exchanged, after his marriage, from the Guards into the Line; he was very poor, since he had nothing but his pay, and never again left India. Well, his wife and the eldest boy died there, and then he sickened of that fatal fever, leaving no child but this, the second son, who had been sent over to England to keep him from the dangerous climate. He had been for years under the charge of his mother's relatives—the Meanwells—and it was not until Edmund on his death-bed wrote earnestly to recommend him to Sir Peregrine's care, that any notice was taken of him. It is the only piece of weakness on my father's part that I can remember."

"But he is coming home to the Towers now, and for ever, since the tutor is to leave him with us here—some relation, I conclude, by the name?" asked Nellie.

"The Meanwell genealogy does not signify very much," answered Adeline scornfully, "but I believe this person was brother to the boy's mother, and a curate somewhere, and teaches pupils. He has done his best, no doubt, to make his (and our) nephew a worthy member of the low-born race, one of whose members has done us the honour of mixing its blood with that of Conyers. However, this young Darrell must be the baronet one day, and the estates, too, are strictly entailed, so that perhaps it is as well to try to give the boy some of the polish of a gentleman."

"I hope, for my part, that we shall be friends; and I feel sure you will learn to like him, Adeline, in spite of your pre-judice," said Nellie; "a lonely lot his has been, poor child, left an orphan so early; and then, as you know, it is for him that the doom that hangs over our house is chiefly to be dreaded. I am sure the thought of it weighs on papa's mind; and I am sure, too, that he has never ceased to suffer from the remembrance that his own only son died among strangers—and unforgiven. He is too proud to show it, but——"

"He is too proud to feel it," returned the elder sister, with flashing eyes.

"Hush!" interrupted Nellie, "here he comes—here is our father."

The door opened as she spoke, and Sir Peregrine Conyers, a tall, spare man of sixty, entered. He had a riding-whip in his hand, and the two dogs that followed him, and now stood lolling out their scarlet tongues, were panting and weary, as if they had had enough to do to keep at the heels of their master's horse.

"Has the carriage returned from Redbridge station?" said the owner of Crag Towers.

"Not yet, papa. We have been expecting it for an hour or more," answered Nellie, while the elder sister's lip curled slightly as she heard the question and the reply; and both girls felt that their father, always a reserved man, had purposely avoided making any personal allusion to his grandson, or mentioning his name.

"We were just speaking of it," said

Nellie; "I think they cannot fail to arrive soon now; unless indeed the constant rains that we have had of late have rendered our home-road too heavy for the carriage, in which case they would have gone round. But I think I hear wheels."

There was a minute of hushed expectancy; next a suppressed sound of feet and voices; and then the door opened, and "Mr. Darrell Conyers" was announced. The door closed softly behind the new comer, and a handsome boy, of some twelve years of age, came fearlessly forward into the room. He was dressed in deep mourning, which contrasted oddly with his bright, frank face, and the sunny curls that clustered thickly about his well-shaped head. After a moment's hesitation, the boy stepped briskly across the wide expanse of carpet that intervened between himself and Sir Peregrine. "I am so glad to see you, grandpapa," he said, with outstretched hand.

"Nay. It is for me, I think, Darrell, to

"No," answered Darrell, "my tutor is
a shy man, and felt, I think, a little nervous
at first seeing our family. He is making
himself very busy, and getting in everybody's way, outside."

An almost imperceptible smile flickered
on the baronet's grave face as he laid his
hand on his grandson's shoulder, and in
somewhat of a kinder tone said, "Well,
heaven bless you, since you are come
among us, my boy, and may the doom of our
house be averted from your young head."

Nellie's gentle eyes filled with tears at
this unwonted sign of emotion on the part
of her father, usually so stern in his self-
control; but Adeline murmured to herself,
"I hate the boy; I knew I should;" while
her cold, fair face wore an expression as
much akin to a sneer as could be borne
by one so lovely, as she turned scornfully
from her nephew.

"Mr. Meanwell" was next announced,
and a tall, raw-boned personage, whose
crumpled black was relieved by a white

necktie, came shambling into the room, and made his awkward salutation in answer to the urbane greeting of Sir Peregrine. It was, indeed, the nature of the Reverend Mark Meanwell to be awkward; and as he stood, with his stooping shoulders and large feet, apologetic as it were for the incongruity of his presence in the midst of so many evidences of wealth and refinement as were there collected, there was something almost piteous in his bashfulness. Yet, plain as were the tutor's features, and ungainly as were his movements, the expression of his homely face was not unpleasing, and even his embarrassment seemed excusable in a studious, quiet man suddenly dragged from his books and his solitude.

"I have much for which to thank you, Mr. Meanwell, in the great care which you have evidently devoted to the education of my grandson. I am glad to be able to congratulate you so sincerely on the apparent result," said the baronet courteously.

It was curious to observe the effect which this complimentary remark had upon him to whom it was addressed. He shuffled his feet to and fro, reddening the while, and began, somewhat irrelevantly, to reply :—"It is not my fault, I assure you, that——"

But here young Darrell interposed with : "You must remember how good and kind you have been to me from the day when I first saw England. I shall never forget it, Mr. Meanwell, I can assure you."

Before the tutor could overcome his timidity sufficiently to be able to reply to this unexpected speech, the loud sound of the gong was heard through the house, and the party dispersed to their several dressing-rooms, and Darrell Conyers and Mr. Meanwell retired under the guidance of Sir Peregrine's valet to the rooms allotted to them.

Thus ended the first interview of Sir Peregrine's grandson with his long estranged relatives, and such was his welcome home.

CHAPTER II.

YOUNG ENGLAND.

THE party that assembled at dinner on the
day of Darrell's arrival at Crag Towers was
by no means of the pleasantest or best
assorted as to its constituents. A more
uncongenial gathering could not easily
have been found than that of this family
group, the members of which had so little
in common with one another. The very
dining-room itself was calculated to exercise
a depressing effect on the spirits of the
Reverend Mark Meanwell, as he adjusted
his napkin and looked furtively at the
unwonted splendours that environed him.
It had not been the ancient castle hall—the
real hall was in the old part of the mansion,
and inhabited by the domestics, who
grumbled sorely at its draughts and ghostly

echoes—but there was armour hanging
on the oak-panelled walls, and branching
antlers of mighty stags slain long ago
alternated with the huge family portraits
in their gilded frames. The great side-
board was loaded with antique and cumbrous
plate, a blaze of heaped-up gold and silver.
There were many lights, but their lustre
was swallowed up, as it were, by the brown
oak that greedily drank in their rays; and
there were many servants, whose tread
made no sound on the thick Turkey carpet
of dull red. The long table itself seemed
disproportioned to the number of the
company, but it was the baronet's good
pleasure that this should be so; and on
ordinary days he took his seat, with his
daughter Adeline, confronting him from
the head of that lengthy board, Nellie
usually sitting alone at her side of the table.
To-day Darrell had been placed beside the
younger Miss Conyers, the Reverend Mark
being disconsolately seated by himself on
the farther side of the mahogany.

The miserable feeling of self-reproachful bashfulness (to describe which we are compelled to borrow the French phrase of *mauvaise honte*, and from which some of the worthiest men suffer the most acutely), weighed very heavily on the meek curate as he went through the ceremony of dinner. He had sense enough to be ashamed of the secret anguish that he could not shake off, but he was painfully conscious of his ill-fitting clothes, and that his hands and ears were very large and red, and his manner of eating clumsy and ungraceful. He felt as if the very servants who changed his plate, or proffered him his choice of beading hock or bubbling champagne, scorned him as they ministered to him. Nor was he able to keep up the ball of conversation as he could have wished to do. Adeline Conyers sat like a beautiful statue of Pride, taking no more heed of the humble visitor than if he had been of painted canvas instead of flesh and blood. Nellie did, indeed, during the first part of the meal, address several

well-intentioned remarks to the tutor, but
merely with the effect of making him blush
and stammer; while Sir Peregrine, who
had strict notions of a host's duties, toiled
in vain to relieve the too evident embarrassment of his guest.

Meanwhile, Darrell, young as he was,
appeared as completely at his ease as the
most consummate man of the world could
have done, and seemed utterly indifferent
to the obvious ill-will of the elder Miss
Conyers, or to the frigid formality of the
baronet. Even Adeline could not but
secretly admire the boy's bearing, under
circumstances which would have made most
of his contemporaries either sheep-faced or
sullen. As it was, his bright bold face
remained unclouded, and Sir Peregrine, who
was no indulgent critic on points of
etiquette, could see nothing at which to
cavil in his grandson's tone or manner.
The boy volunteered no remark, but to
such questions as were addressed to him he
replied with sense and spirit. At length,

giving up the tutor as hopeless, Nellie Conyers turned her attention to her nephew.

"Do you remember India and the coming home, Darrell?" she asked. No inquiry could easily have been more commonplace.

"I remember both quite well," returned the boy, smiling. "The voyage best, perhaps; for I am fond of ships, and of the sea, and enjoyed it amazingly. I had never seen, of course, a vessel bigger than a native boat on a river, but I was very glad to hear I was to be sent round the long way, by the Cape. It was cheaper than the overland, and that was the reason, I believe," he added simply. "But I remember my mother made me promise to be very careful: I mean about playing on the deck, and in the rigging, and that, for fear I should fall overboard—but that you know was a fancy —because of the Doom."

There was an awkward pause. Nellie glanced apprehensively at her father, and

even Adeline raised her haughty head, and
fixed her eyes on the young speaker, who
however went on as if unconscious of the
effect that his words had produced.

"I am not afraid of it," he said, almost
gaily; "and I remember papa was very
much vexed that I should be told of the
Doom, as they called it, and said that it
might make a coward of me. It didn't do
that, I hope; and I am sure it was because
she loved me so fondly that my dear mother
urged me to avoid the water and all that
could lead to my being drowned. She said
this over and over again, before I left India,
and tried to make me believe that the
danger was greater for me than for other
boys."

Here Mr. Meanwell uttered an exclamation of perplexed surprise, and remained
with his mouth open, and a plover's egg,
from the aspic to which he had lately helped
himself, transfixed upon his fork, staring
at his pupil with an intentness that caused
him to forget the eccentricity of his own

behaviour. Darrell was not slow to observe
the curate's self-forgetfulness, or its cause,
and turned kindly, but without a shade
of hesitation, towards him, saying earnestly:
"I see, sir, you are very much surprised
at my mother's having told me, young as
I was, of so terrible a fate. And I fear, too,
that I have startled you by speaking so
suddenly of your sister."

Mr. Meanwell, reddening very much,
uttered an inarticulate reply, and, hastily
conveying the fork to his mouth and
bending his head over his plate, resumed
his meal. The subject might probably
have dropped, had not Sir Peregrine, whose
attention had now been thoroughly aroused,
turned half frowningly towards the tutor.
"Am I to suppose, Mr. Meanwell, that you
did not know of this?" he asked in a tone
of cold courtesy.

"Not in the least, I can assure you, Sir
Peregrine," rejoined the Reverend Mark,
setting down his wine-glass. "My sister—
Mrs. Edmund Conyers, I mean, of course—

did sometimes use expressions in her letters
which——but I never understood them, and
in fact set them down to a mother's natural
apprehensions as to——still I was not prepared to hear that there were any grounds
for——" and here again he broke down
gasping.

"*Do you* know of the legend, Darrell?"
demanded the baronet.

"Yes, sir, I heard the story from my
mother. It was told me, I think, as a
warning to be cautious," replied the boy.

"In that case, I will relate it to you,
Mr. Meanwell," said Sir Peregrine graciously. "You will probably not be sorry to
learn what so intimately concerns the old
family with which your own is now, ahem!
in some degree connected. Nay," he
added with a bow and a grave smile, in
answer to Mr. Meanwell's involuntary
glance towards the servants; "what I am
going to tell you is no secret. A story
that affects the fortunes of the house of
Conyers is, in this neighbourhood, common

property; and this in especial has been talked of around cottage firesides for hundreds of years. Well, sir, you are probably aware that at the time of the Reformation harsh and high-handed things were done in bringing about the suppression of monasteries and the seizure of their lands. Grants were made by the king; and woe betide the members of a religious house who refused to surrender their freehold! Imprisonment, torture, and hanging, or the menace of these strong measures, were certain to convince or to crush such monks as dared to oppose a passive resistance to the royal decrees.

"Among those on whom King Harry bestowed a gift of this sort was a needy courtier, named William Conyers. He was of our name and blood, as you may easily guess, the second son of Sir Gervoyse, who had himself been an only son. He was accounted one of the most reckless gallants of the court, a dicer, a duellist, and utterly unscrupulous in the pursuit of gain or

pleasure. The country people near the
Towers, and the tavern-haunters of London,
equally knew him as Wild Will. There was
consternation in the Abbey of Ouseleigh
when the monks first heard that the estate
had been given to Wild Will Conyers.
Ouseleigh Abbey lies in another county
than this, in Gloucestershire, close to the
estuary of the Severn—the Severn Sea,
as it was formerly called—and where the
breadth of the tidal river is considerable.
It was fairly wealthy, and its rich cornlands
and fat meadows were famous through the
West. The abbot, Nicholas Shepstone,
was an old man of seventy-five, but still
vigorous, and of a stubborn spirit. ' He
may break, but he will not bend, if all be
truth that is told,' had been King Henry's
words when he signed the grant, after a
merry bout of wassail and cock-fighting.
' Then, your Grace, he shall break,' was the
ready reply. Will Conyers had spoken the
truth. He was not one to let conscience or
compunction bar the way to the goal he

had in view; and when he arrived at
Ouseleigh with his men-at-arms, and the
scrivener who bore the parchment with
the royal seal and sign manual, the
arguments he employed were stern and
pressing.

"Abbot Nicholas, as expected, proved
resolute. Not to save limb or life would he
yield up a rood of the monastery possessions. 'Not a pasture, not a croft, not
a coppice,' such were his very words. 'Not
a hand's breadth of the abbey lands will
I cede to the spoiler, were it as worthless
and as barren as yonder waste of yellow
sand that the sea covers twice a day.'

"'Sayest thou so!' answered Wild Will
Conyers; 'then such, lord abbot, shall be thy
sole remaining heritage. Try the venture
as to whether the flood-tide and the salt
waves can be scared from their prey by bell,
book, and candle; and if they relent so will
I.' And he bade his soldiers drive stakes
into the sand, a bowshot below high-water
mark, and caused the abbot, with three of

the principal monks, to be chained to these
stakes, so that, if not delivered, they might
perish by drowning as the tide came up
the estuary. The cruel deed was done, and
soon the tide turned, and in came the grey
sea, flowing up the Severn with a hoarse,
hollow boom of deepening waters; nearer
and nearer came the waves, but still the aged
abbot, bound to the fatal stake, showed no
sign of fear, and the other monks, strength-
ened by the example of their superior,
confronted death without flinching.

"They said it was a piteous and a fearful
sight as the tide rose and rose, until it
reached the captives; and still the scrivener
who stood hard by with his parchment and
inkhorn, offered the pen to the old man's
hand. 'Sign, Abbot Nicholas,' he said;
'sign the surrender, and die a bed-death
within walls. A few minutes and it will be
too late.' But the white-bearded old abbot
did not blench or shudder. 'The Lord
forbid,' he said, 'that I should give the
Church's inheritance to robbers! I am old,

as thou sayest, and so the fitter to die.' And
as the billows foamed around him, he raised
his aged voice in the chant of the Dies Iræ,
in singing which the other monks joined
him, and thus they sang on until the
rushing waters silenced the hymn, and the
voices of those who sang it, for ever. When
the tide ebbed again, they were all found
dead and bound to the stakes, and were laid,
with scanty ceremony, in the abbey vault
that was never again to be a place of burial.
But before Abbot Nicholas died, he said
certain words to the scrivener, in the form of
a message to Will Conyers, who had stood
on the beach above, with his men-at-arms,
jeering at the obstinacy, so he called it,
of the recusants.

"'Tell yonder proud man,' said the
abbot, 'that upon every Conyers of the
old ruthless stock, who shall be, even
as he is, the second son of an only son,
my curse, and the curse of the Church,
and the curse of the poor shall cling as
a garment, and shall not depart. Let them

look to it, I say, lest death by drowning be their doom! As they have sown they shall reap.' Wild Will made light of the abbot's malediction. Nay, he was wont to boast that he bore a charmed life amid all the brawls and plots and perils of that stormy time, and would take the company to witness that he need not fear rapier or poison or the headsman's axe, since his end was to be a watery one. He *was* drowned, however, singular to say, in swimming his horse over the flooded current of the river, some miles from here, one day when a hard-pressed stag had crossed the Wye, and when no other huntsman than he had dared the risk. And then men remembered the abbot's curse. He died unmarried, and Ouseleigh Abbey and its lands lapsed to his brother, my ancestor, and to this day form a valuable outlying portion of the family property—ill got, I admit. Strangely enough, the fate of Wild Will was shared, at long intervals, by two descendants of the Conyers' race, each being, as he was, the

second son of an only son, and the
death of both being like his, by drowning.
One, in Charles the II.'s time, was Eustace
Conyers, a young man of rare promise; the
other, who perished in 1762, bore the name
of William. His portrait hangs in the
gallery above, opposite to that of Wild Will,
and between the two there is a resemblance
that is really remarkable. Hence the origin
of the superstition, or the credence—call
it which you will"—added Sir Peregrine,
with a wave of the hand, "which assigns
an early and a sudden death to every
Conyers whose relationship to the head
of our house fulfils the required conditions.
Darrell, here, is the sole instance of a
second son of an only son, in the Conyers'
line for above a century, and it behoves us
to be especially careful, lest the abbot's curse
should be——"

But at this moment Mr. Meanwell, who
had for some time been growing paler and
paler, slid helplessly from his seat, and
dropped fainting to the floor. The baronet,

who was quite unprepared for this un-
accountable result of the narrative, broke
off abruptly in his discourse and sat aghast.
Nellie uttered an exclamation of pity,
while Adeline Conyers murmured in a half-
audible tone of disgust, "hydrophobia!" as
she surveyed the prostrate form with a
glance of disdain; and the very servants
appeared to require a moment to shake off
their bewilderment before they hurried to
the assistance of the fallen guest. The
only member of the company who preserved
perfect presence of mind was young Darrell,
who instantly sprang forward to lift Mr.
Meanwell's heavy head and support it on
his knee.

"It is nothing, grandpapa," he said
eagerly, but in a tone of conviction. "I am
so sorry, indeed. Perhaps I should have
told you my tutor is subject to fainting fits.
They never come to anything serious, and
there is only one thing to be done for him,
which is to put him to bed and leave him
to himself till the next morning. The

chances are that he will have forgotten all about it; but perhaps I ought to have mentioned it beforehand."

There was a low hum of voices, as sundry of the traditionary remedies for syncope were deferentially suggested by the older servants, while the cause of all this turmoil, the Reverend Mark Meanwell, lay gasping like a great fish freshly caught, with his eyes closed and a livid pallor about his lips. Not for long, however, for very soon the boy's confidence in his own judgment bore down the feeble opposition of those around him, and the tutor—his white necktie having been duly loosened—was carried off, still speechless, to bed.

"I ought to know what should be done," said Darrell coolly, as he resumed his seat. The doctor always recommended quiet and rest for the night after these attacks, but I am very sorry that this one should have been brought on, as I suppose it was, by the journey."

Sir Peregrine, who had winced a little

at the word "grandpapa," could not but
look with somewhat of admiration on the
fearless boy, who of all present was the least
discomposed by the late awkward incident.
Mere child though he was, he had, as if
unconsciously, given proof of an innate
capacity for that rarest of all accomplishments, the power to command without
preferring any distinct claim to obedience.
There was perhaps no quality that more
directly commended itself to the old man's
proud heart than this. "Conyers to the
back-bone!" he muttered behind his wine-
glass, and then bit his lip as if in vexation
with himself for being so prompt to praise
this long-neglected scion of the old race, the
orphaned heir of the rebellious son who
had died unforgiven. The residue of the
party finished their dinner almost in silence.
The gloom had deepened manifestly since the
tutor's ill-timed indisposition had interrupted
the frigid ceremonial of a banquet where
love was not and whence good-fellowship
was excluded. Of the four who remained at

table young Darrell was decidedly the most at his ease. Miss Conyers, cold, haughty, and beautiful, felt her own studied impassiveness to be trite and artificial when compared with the bearing of the nephew whom she already detested. Sir Peregrine began to experience the odd sensation of having met with a stronger spirit than his own in this boy, on whom must one day devolve the wealth and the position that were his birthright. Nellie, whose gentle heart had softened towards the fatherless child, who was so abruptly transplanted to scenes and associations widely differing from those of his earlier years, felt that her kindly-meant advances availed little with a nature so bold and self-reliant.

Long after his daughters and his grandson had left him to sip his claret alone, Sir Peregrine sat with a knitted brow, pondering deeply, as memory conjured up before him many a half-forgotten reminiscence connected with his dead son. How like the boy was to him, and yet how strangely

unlike! There was a great resemblance, so
far as features went, and Edmund, too, had
been frank and outspoken—too much so,
indeed, to please his imperious father—but
there was an undefinable expression in
Darrell's face that had been lacking in that
of Captain Conyers. He was handsomer
too by far; but the main distinction between
father and son was evidently one of
character; nor was the baronet physiognomist enough to read at sight that of his
grandchild. He had reason to be pleased.
Of that there was no doubt, for the boy had
more than answered his expectations. Here
was nothing of what Sir Peregrine had
dreaded, no outcropping of the blood of the
plebeian Meanwells, no homely manners
to be painfully unlearnt, no clownish habits
which it might hereafter prove hard to
eradicate. And yet it may be that the old
man's heart would have been warmer
towards a grandson less free from blame or
blemish, with more of childish timidity and
of childish self-consciousness. We often

love those best who cling to us the most closely for support.

Then, too, Sir Peregrine had drawn a mental portrait of his grandson, and was disappointed—as we almost always are disappointed at finding how very indifferent a limner the imagination has turned out after all. The young heir of his fancy had been less bright, less bold, inferior in grace and in beauty to the original, but at the same time softer and more malleable—plastic material that the baronet could mould according to his judgment. Darrell seemed scarcely the stuff to be moulded. It might be that he was of precisely such a nature as, to Sir Peregrine's thinking, the heir-apparent of the house of Conyers should be; but the present lord of Crag Towers would not have the satisfaction that he had looked for, in forming a pupil of whose proficiency he should have reason to be proud. He rose at last, sighing, from his reverie, and retiring, as was his custom, to the library—a spacious and well-lighted room, where the lamp and candles burned brightly, and whither his favourite dogs followed him unreproved, as they leaped whiningly up, and strove, canine courtiers as they were, to kiss his hand—was seen no more that evening.

The hours which Darrell, in company with his two young aunts, passed in the drawing-room, went somewhat heavily by. Miss Conyers settled herself in her favourite chair, and read a novel with as serene an indifference to her youthful kinsman as though she had been unaware of his presence. The burthen of sustaining the conversation fell upon Nellie, who did her best to find topics likely to interest the new comer.

"How long is it, Darrell, since you came to England?" she asked.

"I have been here for some years—five, it must be—yes, five;" answered the boy; "for I was but seven then, and quite a little fellow. I was a sickly child, you know, and papa was afraid to keep me in that climate.

My brother died there, so it is not to be
wondered at. Yes, I spent five years with
uncle—I mean Mr. Meanwell—and he has
been very good to me. I am quite strong
now, thanks!" he added laughingly, in
reply to a half-mechanical inquiry from
Nellie.

"I hope you are, dear, and glad to come
home," rejoined the younger Miss Conyers.
Her sister's cold eye, as these words were
uttered, rested for a moment on the boy.
Her glance met his, and was quickly averted;
while Nellie was fairly at a loss how best to
entertain the future master of Crag Towers.
Other boys whom she had known had been
voluble on ponies, and hare-hunting, and
cricket-scores, and foot-ball, and perch-fish-
ing; but it could hardly be supposed that
Darrell, not brought up at a public school,
or reared in the ease and opulence of a
country mansion, would be well versed in
the details of athletics or field-sports. And
of his actual tastes and habits she knew
nothing. "Was he fond of study—of reading?" she asked, at length.

"I like reading—novels, that is"—he
answered, looking at the fair questioner as if
he were fitter to patronise her than she
him; "but I'm afraid I'm not at all a
pattern scholar. It is not Mr. Meanwell's
fault if I blunder in my Latin, and know
less of Greek than I do of French. I have
picked up a trifle of French and German
somehow, and that, with the few scraps of
Hindustani that have not slipped my
memory as yet, make up all I know. My
tutor tried to make me as learned as himself, but I fear I was but an idle pupil. By-
the-by," he added, as if a new thought had
occurred to him, "I think I had better go to
Mr. Meanwell now. I can peep in without
disturbing him, poor old boy! and see that
he is going on well, and wants for nothing.
Ten to one that I find him still sound asleep,
and that he will be as fresh as a rose on
waking. So, if you please, Aunt Nellie, I
will say good-night to you both."

Nellie kissed him again, while the elder
Miss Conyers, finding that a slight inclina-

tion of the head was not accepted as a sufficiently affectionate form of parting for the
night, gave him the tips of her jewelled
fingers to shake, and immediately resumed
the perusal of the volume that she held.

"What do you think of him—of them—
Adeline?" asked the younger of Sir Peregrine's daughters, half timidly, when her
nephew was gone. "Is not Darrell's face
handsome—we might say beautiful, if it
were a girl's face; and he seems much more
of a gentleman than those Neville boys,
or young Lord Fitzharry, for instance, in
spite of all the drawbacks of his education,
poor child. Yes, we all ought to be proud
of him; and as for that poor, worthy Mr.
Meanwell——"

"Your amiable optimism, Nellie, is really
too trying for the nerves," interjected
Adeline scornfully, drumming on the floor
with her small foot. "No, I am not
pleased with this precious importation that
you belaud so absurdly. A boy a hundred
years old, and a tutor afflicted with hydro-

phobia! Children, I think, should be children. We have talked sufficiently of this one, and it is growing late. Come! we may as well go to bed, and finish this wearisome day."

CHAPTER III.

ALL MINE.

"ALL mine ! meadow and cornfield, woodland and garden, park and lake—mine—all mine, one day. This is a fair inheritance. The old house, too, how grand it looks in the early sunlight, with its towers and its turrets rising from among the rocks, and the flag floating overhead. He did very well for those who came after him—that old Norman ancestor who built the castle and founded the family. Often as I have seen the place in my dreams I never saw it one half so beautiful as what I see now."

Such was the soliloquy of Darrell Conyers, as he stood at the open window of his chamber, leaning out and gazing upon the lovely prospect that lay spread before him in the

early stillness of that summer morning. The
rapid stream of the Wye went swirling past,
washing the rocky platform on which the
mansion stood, and so near that, from
Darrell's window, a plummet could easily
have been dropped into the rippling river
beneath. Beyond the pebbly shoals, the
silvery shallows, the pellucid streaks of deep
water that sped, arrow-swift, on, amidst
boulders of fretted stone and trailing tan-
gles of dank weed, were to be seen the rich
meadows on the further bank, the browsing
kine, the leafy elms, the feathery hazel
coppice beyond, and the line of uplands
waving with the tender green of the yet un-
ripened corn. To the left rose in imposing
grandeur the group of towers, mingling with
the bold rocks that raised their pinnacles in
many a fantastic shape, of the older or castellated portion of the mansion, once a
stronghold to bridle the wild Welsh. From
the summit of the flag-turret there already
flapped its gaudy folds in the breeze a
banner bearing the Conyers blazon, a cog-

nizance well known in many a battle-field of England's earlier days. To the right could be seen a part of the garden with its lawns and flower-beds, and farther yet, a corner of the park, behind its tall deer-paling, and the gigantic trees encircling the glistening waters of the mere, on which a squadron of snowy-breasted swans rode majestically at anchor.

Little, probably, had the original Lords Marchers, who justly prided themselves on the strong position of their frontier falcon's nest, cared for the picturesqueness of the view from their narrow casements, jealously barred with iron. Nevertheless the castle commanded one of the fairest prospects in England, where the swift Wye rushed through the midst of fretted rocks and rustling woods, varied by green pastures and cornlands. The large bed-chamber at the south end of the house, which had been assigned to Darrell, opened directly into a cheerful morning-room, handsomely furnished in blue silk, and the windows of

which overlooked the wide expanse of the
park itself, with its stately timber, its bosky
coverts and ferny dells, whence peered forth
many a pair of branching antlers, as the
couchant deer lay lazily in the dew-bespan-
gled grass. The sun shone impartially on
the gold-green of the oaks and the huge
limbs of the sycamores, on the black spinnies
of firwood, the terraced lawns, the swelling-
hills, the shining surface of the broad cool
lake, with its tiny islets, its floating swans,
and the masses of reed and bulrush that
sheltered the shy moorhen and the greedy
pike.

Darrell went from room to room, gazing
forth at intervals, as if his interest in the
view could never be fully sated; and then
resuming his survey of the interior of the
apartments which were now his own. They
had belonged once to his father, that
Captain Conyers who was never to derive
much solid benefit from his heirship; and
since the day when he left the castle for the
last time they had not been occupied until,

by Sir Peregrine's orders, they had been
opened for the reception of a new inmate.
It is only a rich man who can afford himself
the fanciful luxury of rooms shut up and
severed from common use, because of some
association that pertains to them. With
the mass of mankind it is not so, the same
walls receiving the blithe young bride that
have heretofore been the last objects on
which have rested the dim eyes of the dying.
Crag Towers, at any rate, was spacious
enough to allow of the sequestration of more
than one suite of apartments; and, since the
final estrangement between father and son,
these had been so set apart.

There were memorials enough in those
rooms of the former occupants. There stood
the desk, ink-stained and hacked with pen-
knives, on which he had scrawled his earliest
letters from school. Those books on the
shelf had been his little library. In a
corner were stacked whips and canes, spears
and fishing-rods, just as their former owner
had left them. Two guns and a regimental

sword hung above the chimney-piece in one
chamber. On the walls of the other were
some half-dozen sketches, rough but spirited,
from the pencil of that same Edmund whose
son was now the successor to his position
and to his ultimate rights. How ghostly
such waifs and strays of the past are apt to
look, even to careless eyes, telling as they
do of hopes long baffled, and day-dreams
never destined to fruition. But Darrell
Conyers, softly whistling the while, in-
spected these inchoate works of art with no
very visible emotion :—" This was his room,
—so the old servant told me—and he was
a boy here, as I am," was his self-communing, as he looked around. " Did he
often think of the old place, I wonder, and of
all he had given up, when he was far away.
I think I should have done so." And again
he stepped to the open casement near him,
and looked out, with somewhat of the air of
proprietorship, on the pleasant landscape
and the many evidences of wealth that surrounded him.

It was a day on which Crag Towers and
the pretty country adjacent were seen perhaps at their best. The Wye was full in
flood; the sky was of a pale bright blue,
dappled by a few white tiny clouds, and the
breeze was stirring freshly among the leaves.
Even the heavy rains that had been frequent of late had contributed to the beauty
of the scene by enhancing the emerald green
of the pastures, while here and there lin-
gered shallow sheets of water, miniature
lagoons, that flashed like burnished silver in
the sunshine. And still the youthful gazer's
thoughts, if not his lips, repeated with a
sort of deliberate exultation the words, "All
mine; my very own; to have and to hold."
There was nothing unnatural in this, perhaps; for the sense of property, be it only in
a broken toy or a scrap of ribbon, is to the
full as strong among children as in maturity.
But this was something more than mere
boyish delight in good fortune. Somewhat
more of resolve there seemed to be in the
steady outlook of those bold blue eyes, in

the tightening of the firm, well-shaped mouth, somewhat more of care about the broad brow, than appeared wholly appropriate to the situation.

The circumstances of Darrell's infancy might, perhaps, have combined to make him more thoughtful, and possibly more tenacious, than were his contemporaries. His father had been banished from the very house that for the first time sheltered the son's head, and had lived and died a needy man, after a childhood lapped in luxury, and bright with the promise of what the world values the most highly. The young heir was quick-sighted enough to note that those on whose capricious bounty he was now thrown could scarcely, at the outset, forgive him the offence of his birth—the fact that in his veins the blood of the humble Meanwells mixed with the haughty ichor of the Conyers' stock, and that the law which secured to him his rights, was really his best friend in default of the instinctive yearnings of affection. Was he thinking, half resentfully, of his father's exile and death: of how his mother had pined, slowly and surely fading in the sultry air of the yellow Indian plains, as an English floweret withers under the fierce sun of Bengal? Or was he taking thought how best he should steer his course; confronted as he was by the undisguised hostility of a near kinswoman, and conscious that by the baronet himself he was accepted as a necessity, rather than hailed as one whose natural place was beneath that stately roof tree? If so, he soon shook himself free of the unwelcome train of thought; and when a servant came to his door to announce the breakfast hour, there was no trace of care or doubt to be seen in the expression of his fair young face.

Breakfast—in most English country mansions a meal that contrasts agreeably with the solemn splendours of the evening banquet—was, even at Crag Towers, less dismally ceremonious in character than had been the dinner of the previous day. Sir Peregrine seemed in an unusually gracious mood, as if his angular mind had been attuned into harmony with the sunny June morning; and the politeness with which he received the tutor's blundering apologies for his "awkwardness" of yesterday evening, was quite in the best style of Louis XIV. Poor Mr. Meanwell, who, if he did not precisely look (as Darrell had predicted) "as fresh as a rose," was, at any rate, as red as one, had come downstairs under convoy of his quick-witted pupil, and seemed in perfect health, but seriously distressed and annoyed at what he called his "absurd behaviour" of the night before. His bashful penitence was so manifestly genuine, that the baronet's manner towards him grew perceptibly more genial; while Nellie, who had liked him from the first, was not sparing in the expression of her sympathy. Only Adeline, frigid and contemptuous as before, preserved the same bearing towards the poor curate that she had assumed from the outset.

"I shall have great pleasure, Mr. Mean-well, in showing you, should you wish it, whatever in the house and grounds may seem best worthy your notice," said Sir Peregrine after breakfast; and the Grand Monarque himself, when offering to conduct some gold-compelling farmer-general around Marly or Versailles, could scarcely have spoken in a tone of more sublime con-descension. The baronet's august courtesy, like a royal invitation, was clearly meant to be taken as a command, and Mr. Meanwell bore his social martyrdom as meekly as many a visitor of lowly pre-tensions had done, under similar circum-stances, before him. After all, it is but a dubious pleasure that a needy guest of frugal habits can derive from traversing lengthy picture galleries, from the walls of which frown or smirk upon him the portraits of bygone ancestors, male and female, of his host; from viewing acres of

glass-roofed mould, where grapes and pines
and rare exotics simmer in a semi-tropical
temperature; or from inspecting a stable
full of noble horses, satin coated and steel-
muscled, and which, as they turn their intelligent heads towards the intruder, appear
to share the stud-groom's covert scorn for
the greenhorn who probably never in his
life owned or mounted a thoroughbred.

Such was especially true of the north-
country tutor, to whom a horse was as
a hippogriff—a highly respectable animal,
with considerable capabilities for work or
for mischief, but with which his desire to
improve his acquaintance was, to say the
least of it, lukewarm. And for the rest,
the very grandeur of Crag Towers, with
its armour, its marbles, its tapestry, the
richly furnished rooms, where now no one
ever slept, or mourned, or made merry as
of old, depressed his spirits. What did
he know of all the extraordinary flowers,
introduced under long names in barbarous
horticultural Latin by the high-salaried

gardener-in-chief, or of the reasons why an
army of subordinate florists were shaving
the velvet lawns, clipping the luxuriant
shrubs, crushing down the glistening gravel,
and taming Nature herself as some hoyden
at a boarding-school might be rendered
conventional by the aid of stocks and back-
board? But he was quite capable of appre-
ciating the sylvan beauty of the park, where
the giant oaks were dressed in all the
bravery of their gold-green foliage, where
there were exquisite little dells, the thick
fern overarched by the interlocking branches
of the hawthorns, and where lake, and up-
land, and thicket, the stately deer, and the
huge carp that flapped among the water-
lilies, seemed to vie in their several claims
on his attention.

Far different was the effect which the
exhibition of all these costly accessories of
country life had produced on the boy who
walked beside him, lending a willing ear
to all that fell from the lips of Sir Peregrine
or of his several dependants.

"You may as well come, too, Darrell,"
the baronet had said, and his grandson
had shown himself so quick an observer,
and also—a rarity at his age—so good a
listener, that Sir Peregrine, by insensible
degrees, found himself addressing his expla-
nations to the boy rather than to Mr.
Meanwell, whose very anxiety to conciliate
made him a sorry victim to so dignified
a cicerone as the master of Crag Towers.
Darrell himself, an object of not unnatural
curiosity to the servants and hangers-on
of the great establishment over which he
would one day preside, examined every
detail of the luxurious paraphernalia which
the magician Wealth conjures up around
his dwelling, with a keen and unflagging
interest. That he should be pleased with
the horses and dogs, the game and the
boats, was no more than Sir Peregrine had
expected. No lad of his age could have
seen unmoved the bright-plumaged pheasants moving lazily among the fir-bolls;
the thymy banks alive with brown-coated

rabbits; the pinnace on the lake, with white
sails and fluttering flag, moored amidst a
flotilla of punts and skiffs; the silken-eared
retrievers, the wiry greyhounds, the array
of nets, guns, and fishing-tackle in the
keeper's lodge. But youth does not often
care for memories of the past, yet here was
a boy whose eye brightened and whose
colour rose when the old baronet pointed to
a rising mound called, locally, Welshmen's
Hill, since there had been, in Glendower's
time, the camp of the last white mantles
that ever beleaguered Crag Towers, and told
how the siege had been raised, when all
hope of rescue had died out, by a desperate
and successful sortie of the English garrison,
led by the Conyers of that day.

Altogether, Sir Peregrine came back to
the house in good-humour with the world in
general, and especially well pleased with
his grandson. This last result was partially
due, perhaps, to the manifest satisfaction
with which keepers, and gardeners, and
grooms had regarded the young heir.

Servants are severe judges of the bearing
and mien of their superiors in station; and
Sir Peregrine Conyers, who would have
wrathfully resented the suggestion that he
was in any degree influenced by such very
humble public opinion as that of his stipend-
iaries, had, nevertheless, secretly shrunk
from the comments that would be passed
on the raw, ill-mannered lad whom he had
expected to receive beneath his roof. Now
Darrell was a boy of whom it was impossible
to be otherwise than proud, and accordingly
the baronet's feelings grew very friendly
towards the brother of the young woman
who had been presumptuous enough to
marry his son.

"I consider myself your debtor, Mr.
Meanwell," said Sir Peregrine very handsomely, when the hour of the tutor's de-
parture arrived, and when the carriage
which was to convey him to the station had
come round to the front; "as your debtor,
for the very great attention which you
have evidently bestowed upon the welfare

and instruction of my grandson, your pupil
and, ahem! nephew!" This last clause,
rapidly slurred over as it was, seemed to
leave a bitter after-taste on the lips of the
courtly speaker, but in an instant he
resumed: "I thank you, sir, in my own
name and in that of the family, for bringing
to us one apparently so worthy to be hereafter its chief, and shall always entertain
towards yourself personally the most lively
sense of gratitude and esteem. One part of
my obligation, and that the smallest, I will
endeavour to discharge." And, as he spoke,
the baronet thrust into the tutor's red-
knuckled hand an oblong slip of paper, one
of those slips the stiff crispness of which
tells its own tale. But Mr. Meanwell, who
had changed colour more than once, and
had shuffled his large feet awkwardly to and
fro, like those of an amiable bear preparing
to dance a saraband, during his host's discourse, politely but distinctly declined to
take Sir Peregrine's money. Nothing, he
said, was due to him. He had been paid,

by remittance from India, the stipulated
sum for Darrell's tuition and maintenance
during the full period of the boy's residence with him, and he wanted no more.
He was very much obliged by Sir Peregrine's kind intentions—yes, he would glance
at the cheque, if it were wished, but
the amount, princely as he owned the
present to be, could not make him swerve
from what he had said—but really he could
not accept it.

The baronet was half inclined to be
offended. Magnates such as he do not like
to have their gifts forced back upon them;
and Sir Peregrine scarcely knew what to
make of a needy curate's refusal of a draft
for some hundreds of pounds. But his
better nature prevailed, and he shook Mr.
Meanwell very cordially by the hand,
saying, "My good opinion, sir, at least
you cannot decline."

Darrell's bearing, as he bade farewell to
his old tutor, was, of its kind, perfect, pupil
and pedagogue seeming alike to ignore or to

forget the fact of their relationship, but each
evincing a genuine liking for the other.
"Good-bye, sir; pray write to me sometimes,
and do not forget me, or our pleasant days
together. I shall always think of you," said
the boy, as Mr. Meanwell stepped into the
carriage, and the footman closed the door.
It would scarcely have been unbecoming, at
his age, if the young heir had shed a tear or
two on parting with his early instructor and
near relative, from whose charge he had
passed under that of those who, although
akin to him in blood, were as yet mere
strangers. But Darrell's eyes, as one or
two of the lynx-visioned servants observed,
were dry. "A hard-plucked one is young
master; you may take your oath of it,"
said Mr. Vickers, the stud-groom, in confidence to Sir Peregrine's elderly valet. It
must have been pure curiosity that brought
so important a functionary, the Minister of
the Equine Department, personally to super-
intend the start of the third-best bays and
the double brougham, bound to the railway

station with so uninteresting a live cargo as
a gawky curate who begged pardon of everybody on his blundering route.

But, indeed, Darrell's buoyant spirits
seemed incapable of depression. Far from
moping, as so many of his years would have
done, the future head of the house of
Conyers became every hour more thoroughly
at home in the midst of his unaccustomed
surroundings. Sir Peregrine himself secretly
marvelled at the frank and graceful simplicity with which this mere child seemed to
disarm criticism, winning as if unconsciously
the respect and goodwill of all who fancied
that they saw in him the budding promise
of a richly gifted manhood. And thus, not
unpleasantly, some days passed by.

CHAPTER IV.

BY THE MILL.

MIDSUMMER nights are short, and the days at the same joyous epoch are proportionally long, yet the hours of working wakefulness vary in country places according to the degree of the employer. Farmer Pottles, who likes to meet Aurora face to face, would growl out many a profane oath if he could not get his blinking men afield long before the hinds who cultivate the Squire's acres, or till Sir John's or his Grace's expensive home farm, had sallied forth from the shelter of their thatched cottages. Thus, although labour had begun in sundry portions of the parish, the grounds, gardens, park, paddock, and meadows about Crag

Towers were as yet utterly deserted when Adeline Conyers noiselessly opening a glazed side-door that led into what was called the Lady's Garden, traversed the narrow paths with a light but resolute tread, caring to all appearance as little for the odorous wealth of the rose-bushes that grew in lavish luxuriance around her as for the pearly dew that clung to leaflet and grass blade, as if Night's parting caprice had been to sprinkle the country side with tiny diamonds. Something of suspicion, some vague taint of blame, commonly attaches itself to those who are seen abroad at untimeous hours. And in this respect the harsh judgment of the world is not seldom right. Of course it is quite possible to be afoot on a legitimate and even praiseworthy errand when the vast majority of mortals are sound asleep. But when such sallyings forth are of an obviously furtive character, when the exertion or sacrifice of rest and ease which they require contrasts with the habits of the person principally concerned, the motive cannot readily be assumed to be a creditable one.

Miss Conyers had chosen her time well. She was clear of the house, of the grounds, of the demesne, before any prying eyes had the chance of setting busy brains and tattling tongues to speculate on the conduct of Sir Peregrine's eldest daughter. Yet she was not so outrageously matutinal as to become the target of criticism on the return from her excursion. When she came back, gardeners, weeding boys, woodmen, and gamekeepers would see her, no doubt, but without knowing how long or how far she had strayed from home. Once away from the immediate neighbourhood of the mansion, and on the free high road, she walked briskly on past orchard and meadow, while high overhead rose the leafy hedge-rows, gay, at that season, with the long trailing branches and neglected blossoms of the white wild rose.

Adeline, in the midst of the luxuriant surroundings of her stately home, seemed

quite another being from the Adeline who
now passed swiftly on along the empty
highway, the dust of which was as yet un-
disturbed by wheel or hoof, up green lanes
overshadowed by oaks that murmured pleasantly as the breeze stirred their young
leaves, past thatched cottages that were
half hidden by the high palings and garish
marigolds and heavy-headed sunflowers of
the garden in front. Her indolence, her
careless scorn for all that moved the
anxiety of others, the proud composure of
her demeanour, had vanished as if by
magic. There was a watchfulness in her
bright eyes, a resolute firmness about her
clear cut lips, such as very few had ever
seen there; while her very tread, rapid and
elastic, had in it somewhat of the stealthy
agility of the panther that prowls for prey.

Arrived at a green spot where cross-roads
met, and where a white guide-post pointed
with one carved finger towards a narrower
lane than the other three, while on the slip of
wood could faintly be discerned the weather-

beaten inscription, "To Gridley Green, Lock Gate, and Pounder's End," she halted for a brief space, and drawing forth a letter, the seal of which had long since been broken, unfolded the paper, and read over slowly, not for the second, third, or fourth time, the contents, which were as follows:—

"MADEMOISELLE,

"Pardon, a thousand times pardon, I pray of you, the freedom which I thus take to derange you from your tranquillity. Necessity, hélas! as your English proverb so fitly tells us, knows no law, and at the call of duty we must all be ready to make sacrifice of one sort or other. Mine is made, even now, in that, at my age, with my broken health, in my old days, I leave my country to undertake so long a voyage. But I do it willingly, of light heart, to serve where I love. Our former correspondence will have prepared you in part, chère Mademoiselle Conyers, for my presence so

near you, and of my desire to gratify your
wish judge by the promptness with which I
have pressed myself to come across sea and
land to your brumous country. But all this
can be told much better by tongue than by
the pen. Circumstances preventing me
from having the honour to present myself
at your distinguished home, may I ask of
your complaisance, dear lady, to meet me
near Gridley Green, at the great morning
before the rustic *badauds*—for, believe me,
our good villagers are sad gossips—are
astir. I stay at the little *auberge*—inn, as
you others say—the *Conyers Arms*, but
better not make wonder the people more
than must be. The mill just outside,
where the stream runs, is much quieter,
and if you will condescend to find yourself
there on Wednesday, Mademoiselle, say
towards half-past six, you will confer an
additional favour on one who asks you
to receive the assurance of her high consideration.

"VEUVE TRACRENARD."

Adeline Conyers, as she deliberately re-
perused this singularly-worded epistle, would
have been worthy of the attention of one
of those mighty limners of the past, beneath
whose potent brush human passion was transferred to a deathless canvas. The icy crust of
cold, impassive pride was for the moment
broken, and the fierce volcanic fires that
lurked unsuspected beneath leaped luridly
up and threatened to burst forth from their
restraining bounds. She looked beautiful
still, but with a fierce and unholy beauty, as
she scanned the manuscript which she held,
and of which every word was already firmly
impressed upon her memory. It was evident that, polite and even obsequious as
was the dictation of the letter before her
eyes, she fully understood the peremptory
nature of the summons, and that she
bitterly resented the call which she had not,
nevertheless, ventured to resist. "Time
was," she murmured to herself, with a
slight but terribly expressive gesture of her
supple, white wrist and tightly clenched

hand, "when it was not so safe, not so
easy, to impose conditions on one of our
name and blood, within so short a ride of
Crag Towers, where armed men were quick
to take up the quarrel of those whose badge
they wore, and at whose table they fed.
The world has altered; grown better, as
they say. Well for you, my foreign friend,
that it is so!" And with glittering eyes
and a low, bitter laugh, she put up the
letter again, and pursued her way.

Presently Miss Conyers, who had by this
time emerged from between the lofty hedges
into a more open tract of country, caught
sight of a grey, old mill, embosomed in the
midst of tall poplar trees that reared themselves aloft like so many quivering green
steeples, some meadows, a brook swollen by
recent rains, and an old bridge of a single
arch spanning the discoloured stream—a
bridge that in many parts of England would
have been built of wood, but which in that
western shire was of greystone, all spangled
with yellow lichens. Some bowshot off,

reckoning the arrow-flight by the liberal old
English measurement of twenty score—a
distance fabulous to modern toxopholites—
appeared the first white cottages of the
long, straggling village of Gridley Green.
On the bridge itself, but so screened by the
high parapet as to be almost invisible, was a
dark something that might or might not
have represented the half-seen outlines of a
human form. Adeline never doubted, but
pressed on till she reached the bridge. Her
conjecture proved to have been correct, for
a shapeless bundle that had taken up its
position on a flat-topped stone, originally
designed as a mounting-block, rose from its
seat as she drew near, and dropped its
curtsy, and grinned its grin of leering recognition. An old woman, sallow, stoutly
built, with fierce black eyes, in which the
fire of the southern nature was tamed and
subdued, as it were, by the long habit of
shrewd self-restraint; with a beak like that of
a bird of prey, and a coarse mouth still well
garnished, in despite of years, with strong

white teeth that could have matched with those of Red Riding Hood's false grandam, the wolf; with iron-grey hair very neatly arranged beneath a bonnet which was old, indeed, but in perfect taste, considering the age of the wearer. So with the woman's other garments, which were crumpled and dulled by use, but well made and of good materials, while the neat boots and tightly fitting gloves showed a lingering trace of that concern for personal adornment that never quite deserts the mature French-woman. Such was in aspect the person, easily identified with the writer of the letter which Adeline had just re-read, who now rose and greeted Miss Conyers with a reverential silence which proved that she did not intend to begin the conversation.

Adeline was the first to speak.

"You have done wrong, madame," she said, in the most trenchant tone of her clear voice, "in coming here—wrong in all respects. There was not, and there is not, the slightest reason for any personal communication between us, and there is always a chance that your presence in this quiet part of the country may excite idle curiosity and comment. Recriminations, however, are worse than useless. Have you brought it ? "

This last question was sharply and severely put. But Madame Tracrenard, if such were her name, made no direct reply to it, but stood rubbing her gloved hands very softly together, and smirking as though deprecating the anger of her former acquaintance.

" Upon my faith," she said at last, " this is a reception chilling enough, after a journey so detestable and a sojourn so *triste*. What have I done, belle demoiselle, but travel, travel, weary leagues to render you a service desired, and you receive this poor Widow Tracrenard as if she had come to steal spoons from your château so superb. Ah, well! I have lived too long to look for gratitude. But how cruel are you grown, beautiful lady, and how hard !

Autrefois, you were more gentle, more trusting, more——"

" Say more credulous, madame, and your words will match better with your thoughts," returned Miss Conyers bitterly; "I am in no mood for trifling, however; so, if you please, we will address ourselves to business considerations only. Have you brought what I desired you to send? "

" How if I tell you no? " answered the Frenchwoman after a pause, and speaking with provoking slowness, while she narrowly watched the beautiful face on which her own glowing eyes were fixed.

Adeline's lip curled scornfully.

" In that case," she said coldly, and half turning as if to go, "there would be nothing to keep me here."

Madame Tracrenard uttered a little chuckling, cackling laugh, impossible to any but a native of Gaul, and muttered something in an undertone about the Porte St. Martin and the footlights.

" How if I tell you yes? " she then said,

with a smile that might have done credit to
an ogress offering hospitality to a belated
bevy of stray children; while all the time
her crafty eyes narrowly watched the proud,
beautiful face on which they had fixed
themselves, as if to mark the effect of her
words. But there was not much to be
learned from such scrutiny, since Adeline's
command of countenance would have done
credit to a Spartan.

"If so," she said quietly, "it would next
be necessary to come to terms."

Madame Tracrenard's laugh this time
was one of genuine enjoyment.

"You are a sensible young lady," she
said blandly; "also is it a pleasure to deal
with one who so well comprehends that the
poor cannot afford to give anything for
nothing—to the rich at least. What re-
compense does mademoiselle's native good-
ness suggest for the exertions and the
charges, the heavy charges—they are Jews,
look you, your English landlords and cab-
men—incurred on her behalf?"

"Strictly speaking," said Adeline, with perfect outward composure, "I owe you nothing. What I now demand ought, as you well know, to have passed into my possession when—when other papers were given up, and it was only by an oversight, perhaps intentional on your part, that this was not the case. I have paid, again and again, amply for all that you have done, for your forbearance, no less than for your acts. I am prepared for some present sacrifice, but it must not be too heavy, for you are mistaken when you account me rich. I am not so, and you must not allow yourself to be dazzled by the glitter of my father's wealth. There is but very little at my disposal, and I am no heiress. I have not your instinct for a bargain, my good foreign friend. How much do you ask?"

The Widow Tracrenard flung open her two well-gloved hands with a gesture that was to all appearance unstudied, but which would have done credit to an actress of the serious drama.

"Nothing!" she exclaimed, "absolutely nothing, that is, if I could listen to the voice of my heart, and did not duty, with imperious mandate, force me to remember that there are others whom it would be a crime to forget, that I am not alone in the world, and have not the right to be generous. Not for my sake, not for that of old Joséphine Tracrenard, but for that of another, now broken in health, alas! and needing much that I can ill supply. I must name my price. Two hundred and fifty pounds sterling."

These last words, in strong contrast with the sentimental phrases that had preceded them, were uttered with a kind of steely snap, like the abrupt closing of a rat-trap.

Miss Conyers looked steadily at the old Frenchwoman, now contemplating her with greedy, glittering eyes, and shook her head slightly, but resolutely.

"Impossible!" she said, and there was a ring of truthfulness in her voice that compelled attention from the listener, "wholly

impossible now. There are, your French
saying declares, two bad bargainer—she who
asks too little and he who holds out for too
much. You will consult your own interests
best, believe me, by being moderate now."

There were unfathomed abysses of cunning in Veuve Tracrenard's greedy eyes as
she listened.

"What, then, does mademoiselle offer?"
she asked, with a dry, little cough. "If it
be forbidden to *marchander*, it is probably
permitted to be curious as to the *chiffre*
proposed."

"All I have to give—all the money that,
without exciting inquiry and suspicion, it
was possible for me to get together," answered Miss Conyers, drawing forth a little
packet of crisp bank-notes—"ninety pounds
in all."

"It is not enough! Ninety pounds,
indeed! *c'est de la ladrerie, ça!*" broke out
the Frenchwoman, with a shrill indignation,
which if not real was at least admirably
simulated! "You mock yourself of me,

dear lady, when you make me so pitiful a
proffer."

There was insolence in the words, in the
tone in which they were spoken, in the
glances and gestures that accompanied them,
such as might well have provoked an angry
retort from one of a far milder nature than
that of the haughty Adeline. But instead
of wrath, it was with a laugh and a bright,
unclouded face that Madame Tracrenard's
speech was received.

"Hark you! good madame," said Miss
Conyers pleasantly enough; "I know as well
as you do, that your rejoinder would have
been the same had I brought with me two
hundred pounds instead of less than one.
You make it a point of conscience to
haggle for high terms, but, believe me, in
this instance it will be useless. Come, old
acquaintance, let us play frankly for once—
cartes sur table! Have I ever approved
myself close-handed in money matters yet?
When I tell you that I can give the sum I
have mentioned, and no more, for what you

have to sell, and for the gratification of my whim, I speak the simple truth. I am willing to pay for my caprice, but risk I will not incur, and without risk I can obtain no further supply of ready cash. Let us agree, or part." And she turned as if to go.

"It is too little! It is a cruel sacrifice! I had spent, in anticipation, every franc of the amount," said Veuve Tracrenard, wringing her gloved hands, but more politely than before.

"Ay, spent or saved," returned Adeline with perfect coolness; "but time wears, and I have far and fast to walk on my way homeward. Let us deal, and say farewell, without more words than are needful. Do not fancy that you are marketing at your stall—in the Halle aux Poissons, or the Marché aux Fleurs, which was it?—as you did before you married that sergeant-major."

"Pardon me," said Widow Tracrenard, drawing herself up, and compressing her lips as she spoke, "Achille got his epaulettes as a sub-lieutenant only a year later, and well he had earned them too against the villainous Bedouins, *là bas.* A superb soldier, six feet, French measure, and *bel homme*, like a lamb, too, for temper!" And the old Frenchwoman actually wiped away a snuffy tear from her hard eyes as she recalled the physical and moral merits of the defunct.

"Have I not seen his portrait with the cross of the Legion hanging from it, and the sword beneath?" said Miss Conyers gently. "And have I not heard how they called you the Belle Bouquetière in old days, and what a winsome couple you looked as you passed in at the door of St. Eustache on the wedding-day? I wish we could remain friends, you and I, but for that we must come to terms, and quickly, or I shall be missed at the Towers. Come, is it arranged?"

"I can refuse you nothing, nothing," whimpered out the widow, as she produced a roll of something wrapped in silver paper. She was softened, really softened, for the moment, by Adeline's gracious manner no

less than by the reminiscences of bygone
happiness which her words had conjured up;
but she was by far too shrewd a woman of
business to allow sentiment to outweigh
solid profit, had she seen her way to improving on the terms that had been offered.
As it was, she yielded. *"Donnant, donnant!"*
she said with an ogreish playfulness, as she
relinquished her hold of the roll, and
clutched and counted the bank-notes.

"I must go now," said Miss Conyers, with
a glance at her watch.

"Have you nothing to send—no word of
remembrance to any?" asked the old
Frenchwoman; then, as if reading the reply
in Adeline's cold gaze, she added, "But we
have no more time for conversation. *Sans
adieu!*" and Madame Tracrenard actually
put up her bony cheek to be kissed, but
Adeline did not heed the gesture, but with
a quiet, "I wish you a good journey,
madame!" turned away, and began to
retrace her steps homewards.

The Frenchwoman stood for some mo-

ments watching the tall, slender figure as it
swiftly moved away, and apparently with
very mingled feelings, to judge from the
various expressions that flitted across her
crafty face; and when it was no longer
visible, pocketed the notes and trudged
slowly but sturdily off in the direction of
the village.

Miss Conyers walked briskly on until the
leafy hedges and the overhanging boughs
of the trees screened her from sight, and
then halted at a point where a brook, now
swollen by the rains, ran babbling past
to join the larger mill-stream. There were
stepping-stones, flat and broad, by which
this thread of brawling water could be
crossed, and on one of these Adeline took
her stand while slowly and with unsteady
fingers she opened the roll of silver paper
and unrolled the sheet of thin cardboard
which it had contained. What met her
eyes was a sketch, spirited indeed, but
somewhat roughly executed, which represented two persons. One was a girl, young,

slender, delicately pretty, who was seated
beside a table on which lay a tumbled heap
of flowers, one hand half hidden by the
roses and lilies, as she looked trustingly up
into the face of him who stood beside her.
A young man, this latter, tall and slightly
built, with long hair tossed back from a face
which, to judge by what could be seen of
the profile, was handsome enough. He
stood leaning on his fair companion's chair,
the back of which his left arm half en-
circled, and his attitude was graceful, but
with a studied grace that had in it something theatrical. This drawing had a
strange interest for Adeline, since, in spite
of her impatience to return to Crag Towers
before her absence should be a theme for
gossip, she gazed at it long and fixedly, as if
the sight of it conjured up dreams and associations which had nothing to do with her
present life. At length she started from
her reverie, and with a rapid fierceness of
action, tore the sketch into a hundred frag-
ments; and tossing the scraps of cardboard

into the brook looked moodily on watching the tiny pieces as they were washed away by the current. Then, with a sigh that seemed wrung from her, half unconsciously, she turned her face homewards and left the place with a swift and hurrying step. Such was her haste, that it was yet very early, in the conventional sense of the word, when she reached the demesne of which Sir Peregrine was master and lord. Fortune had favoured her, for she met neither hind nor gardener as she sped, swiftly and cautiously, by tortuous ways, across the wide pleasaunce.

Yes, it was early yet, and although from the broad lawns came the sounds of labour, as the mowers whetted the keen scythes with which they were about to level the dew-pearled grass blades, no one seemed to be stirring among the dense shrubberies and the luxuriant flower-beds and thickets of standard rose trees, and bushes of purple rhododendron. She had done well that morning, better for herself, probably, than

she had expected. She had gained possession of that which she had wished, and
whatever her motive for its destruction, it
no longer existed. That dumb tell-tale was
blotted for ever out of the world's hoarded
archives. She had got rid also of the
guardian dragon of that coveted prize with
more ease than could readily have been
counted on. Well she knew that it was but
a hollow truce that had been patched up.
between herself and the crafty, covetous old
foreign woman, whose craving for gold made
her in the long run inexorable as a creditor.
But, for the time, an armistice did exist,
and to the young especially a reprieve is
welcome, fraught as the future is with such
possibilities of bright promise. Yes, fortune
had favoured her. She traversed the old-
fashioned rose-garden, entered the mansion,
and regained her own apartments un-
challenged and, to the best of her belief,
unseen.

CHAPTER V.

COMING SHADOWS.

CRAG Towers, like some other ancient
mansions of the same stamp, was rich in
family portraits. The best of these embel-
lished the picture gallery; but there had
been many a bygone Conyers—of the fair
sex in especial—the transferring of whose
features to canvas had employed the brush
of more than one limner. The seven ages of
man, and still more so of woman, might be
seen in that multiplicity of dusky likenesses
that hung everywhere—in state apartments,
on the grand staircase, in the entrance-
hall, or in back rooms and lumber closets—
according to their degree of artistic merit.
There was the laughing boy, the veteran
whose grizzled locks had thinned under

the helmet, the blooming bride, and the
wrinkled crone, a strange similitude running
through the long array of faces; for the
lords of Crag Towers had a strongly marked
type of countenance, and artists, even in
Tudor and Plantagenet reigns, were not
unaware of the mute flattery which an
added touch can impart to the homeliest
features. Adeline Conyers, as rapidly yet
with light and furtive tread she ascended
the stairs, seemed to flinch from the cold,
steady stare of these painted shadows of
the long dead. Simpering shepherdesses in
the Pompadour blue and pink, pursed up
their pretty mouths as she passed before
their gilded frames. Bold-eyed, carmine-
lipped maids of honour, in the costume of
Charles II.'s wicked, witty court, leered on
her as if in saucy scorn. Grim warriors,
in steel breast-plates, scowled their dis-
approval. The very children appeared to
cease weaving rose-wreaths or toying with
their falcons, to gaze inquisitively on her
as she hurried past. Well as she knew that

this was but an illusion of her own heated fancy, yet she was glad when she had left the grand staircase behind her, and gained the west wing, where her own apartments lay.

Safe at last! safe and unseen! She had threaded her way well, swift and silent as the hunted deer that hears the baying of the hounds, and now she was secure from comment or observation. Stay! what was that? Nothing very unusual, certainly— merely the sudden clapping of a door; yet Miss Conyers started and changed colour as she heard it, and looked hastily round. But no; there was no one to be seen, nor was there anything to indicate which door.it might be that had been closed so abruptly, and whether by human agency or by a fitful gust of wind. She was in her own rooms now: the chamber whence she had stolen, a dressing-room that lay beyond, and a larger apartment, furnished in the French fashion, in pink and white silk, such as upholsterers of the Faubourg St. Honoré supplied to their best customers, when the Empire of the Third Napoleon was a span-new sovereignty, but which yet preserved much of its glossy freshness; and she had nothing to apprehend from unwelcome curiosity. Why, then, had her accustomed haughtiness so utterly forsaken her, that as she closed the door her usual stately coldness was exchanged for a careworn, abject demeanour that was almost grovelling in the self-reproachfulness of its humility? What, after all, had she done? She had left the house by stealth, and with precautions that proved how important she deemed it to avoid prying eyes. But had her steps been dogged by any spy the most watchful, surely little to her discredit could have been gleaned from any detail of her interview with Veuve Tracrenard. It must surely have been the exaggerated sensitiveness of a morbid pride that made her shrink so vehemently from the discovery of what would, probably, have been classed as a mere piece of whimsical extravagance.

Yet Adeline Conyers, as she saw her own reflection in the tall pier-glass, and noted the signs of haste in her disordered hair and quick breathing, beheld also a white, terror-stricken face from the sight of which she recoiled as from a blow. That face hers! She frowned and bit her lip in no feigned anger, but the wrath did not subdue the fear that dominated her: a fear none the less potent because its cause was concealed. The sharp, metallic clang, however, as the ornamental clock on the chimney-piece struck the hour, warned her that she had now no leisure for the indulgence of feelings of any sort; and rapidly and dexterously she busied herself in making such changes in her attire as should avert suspicion as to the object of her singular wakefulness. Discreet young ladies of Adeline's degree well know when it is not expedient to make use of the services of their maid; and without any assistance she made herself ready to assume her place at the breakfast table below. No one, not even

a detective, whose business it is to suspect
all fair seemings and to be incredulous of
whatever is plausible, would have picked
out Adeline, when the family assembled,
as the heroine of what might almost be
elevated to the dignity of an adventure.
Cool and self-possessed, she bore the weight
of her secret, whatever it might be, without
a trace of visible emotion.

An incongruous company, in some sense,
it was that gathered each morning around
the breakfast table at Crag Towers; the
moral and mental dissimilarity being heightened, as it were, by the distinct physical
resemblance which seemed as the heirloom
of all who shared the blood of Conyers.
There was the baronet, spare, rigid, almost
stern of speech and bearing, yet with a
certain tenderness of heart and sensitiveness of nature beneath the crust of pride,
which to superficial observers seemed the
one element of his character. There was
Nellie, gentle of spirit, a girl as free from
haughtiness as she was from guile, not

quick to claim even what was justly her own, and yet of whom a shrewd physiognomist might have predicated that she would prove very steadfast to her plighted word or to the course of conduct which she knew to be right. There was her imperious elder sister, queenly of aspect and bearing. And there was Darrell, with his fair, fearless face, the sunny curls clustering around his broad white brow, as round that of a boyish Apollo. Every hour, every day, seemed to confirm the singular ascendency which from the very first this young new comer in the household had exercised over its grave master. A keen observer—and Adeline's powers of observation were very keen—might have noticed that the baronet's looks brightened as his eyes rested on Darrell; that his voice, when he addressed the boy, was softer than was usual with him, and that he who was by no means slow to express his displeasure at the conduct of those over whom he had authority, seldom or never uttered a word that could be construed into a rebuke or admonition where his grandson was concerned.

There was not much of sustained conversation at the morning meal. Nellie, with a glance at the unclouded sky and sparkling sunshine without, did certainly make mention of having been startled upstairs by the loud and sudden slamming of a door; and Darrell instantly averred that he, too, had heard the sound, not very usual in well-ordered establishments such as Crag Towers, where the servants do their ministry as if shod with velvet, and where the domestic machinery of every-day life works smoothly, and without any of that unpleasant jarring which sometimes vexes the patience of less wealthy householders. But Miss Conyers, who had still better cause to remember the occurrence, did not see fit to make public her own experiences in the matter, and the subject was allowed to drop. Sir Peregrine Conyers, as was often the case, was busy with his letters and journals, a pile of which, extracted

from the brass-locked post-bag with the
Conyers' arms stamped in faded gilding on
the seasoned leather, lay beside his cup, and
received the greater share of his attention.
His correspondence, as is usual with men
of his means and station, was eminently
miscellaneous : the puffing prospectus of
a fine new shop or ephemeral company
jostling the blue office paper and formal
handwriting of the family lawyer, and the
portion of the budget which had reference
to business being considerably in excess of
that which related to more personal matters.
There were letters ostentatiously hurried as
to their caligraphy, and endorsed " House
of Lords," " House of Commons," or with
the names of famous London clubs, which
had probably something to do with politics,
for Sir Peregrine's name was a local tower
of strength to his party. There were the
short, blurred notes of old friends, merely
a few awkward words scrawled on paper,
in the atrocious penmanship which was
thought " mons'ous gentlemanly " in the

Georgian reigns, but kindly meant. There was a begging letter, glibly magniloquent, from some professional correspondent, who plied the estated gentry with copper-plate appeals for alms; and there were other missives of a less downright description— begging letters, too, of a sort—fluent and lengthy, and with italics liberally sprinkled over the closely written pages, beseeching Sir Peregrine, for old friendship's sake, to procure for dear Edward and darling Arthur lucrative and creditable employment in Her Majesty's service, civil, military, or diplomatic, and to confer a fresh obligation on the eternally grateful mamma of those meritorious young gentlemen.

The very last letter of the morning's supply was the one which seemed to impress Sir Peregrine the most, for he had scarcely cast his eye over its contents before he looked up, exclaiming in a tone of evident gratification—

"I am glad of that, very glad. Your Cousin Craven, my dear, finds that he is able to accept my invitation, and to pay us a visit here before going to sea again. Indeed, as far as I can understand his words, he expects to be appointed to a vessel of a different class, as his family connections and, ahem! his merits, entitle him to be, and will be for a short time free from duty. He writes from Paris, whither my letter followed him."

Thus spoke Sir Peregrine, and a very various effect was produced upon the auditors of these few words.

Nellie, whose sudden flush of tell-tale colour much increased her natural prettiness, bent down her face and fixed her eyes upon her plate as if to avoid scrutiny; while young Darrell's bright face was for a moment clouded, and in the next expressed the strong impulse of boyish curiosity, coupled with an odd and indefinable under-current of some feeling akin to a subtle enjoyment of suppressed mischief. Miss Conyers, on the contrary, had lifted her beautiful head with somewhat of the

graceful menace of a snake that rears itself
to confront a rash enemy, and there was
almost a defiant look in her glittering eyes,
while her firm red lips were compressed
together. No one spoke, however; and Sir
Peregrine, with a glance of something like
surprise, first at one and then at the other
of his daughters, said, in that half-offended
tone which was frequent with him:

"You do not seem, either of you, pleased
to welcome your cousin?"

"Oh! yes, papa. I am sure we are glad,"
said Nellie, in a low voice, still looking
down.

Sir Peregrine, like most fathers, was not
very observant of his daughters' demeanour;
and when Miss Conyers made some remark,
with her accustomed air of well-bred indifference, concerning her cousin's arrival,
he was perfectly satisfied, and went on
feeding his dogs, one of which had stationed
itself, as usual, on the right and the other
on the left of their master's chair, and in a
leisurely fashion sorting the opened letters.

That he was himself pleasurably impressed by the tidings of his nephew's impending visit was evident.

"Yes, yes," said the baronet, good-humouredly, but without raising his eyes; "a fine, high-principled young man, is Craven Conyers—very different from his poor father, my junior. I don't mean as to the principles, of course," added Sir Peregrine rather hastily, as it occurred to him that the awkwardly sounding sentence appeared to convey a censure on the departed; "but in tastes and habits. The colonel, poor fellow, was inclined to be an exquisite and a dangler in London drawing-rooms and on race-courses; whereas young Craven took to the sea early, and is as manly a lad as any in England."

The baronet did not mention, as he might have done, how heavy a tax on his elder brother's purse and patience had been Colonel Craven Conyers, whose debts he had thrice paid, and than whom no greater scapegrace ever wore the uniform of a

Guardsman. That gentleman's connection
with the army had indeed been nominal
for all the later years of his selfish and
ill-spent life, since he had been thankful
to sell out, and to pass the evening of his
days in Paris, a pensioner on his wife's
income, which had, luckily for her, been
too tightly settled upon her to permit the
principal to fall into the hands of her spend-
thrift husband. The widow still resided in
Paris, and would probably die there. She
it was who had been the godmother and
admiring patroness of Adeline; and from
her house the young sailor had written to
announce his intention of promptly availing
himself of his uncle's invitation. The young
man had always been somewhat of a favourite
with Sir Peregrine, who had never, however,
been quite free from a slight twinge of unacknowledged jealousy when he recalled the
fact that, in the very probable contingency
of his own son and his children succumbing
to the fatal Indian climate, Craven stood
next in succession to the title and lands.

"Yes, Master Darrell," said the baronet, after a pause, almost playfully recurring to the old fear that had haunted him many a time, but which had lost its sting now that his true and natural heir was safe beneath his roof. "If you had died out yonder, as your poor brother did, Craven would only have had to await my death, to be Sir Craven, chief of the house of Conyers, and master of the Towers. Not, to do the lad simple justice, that I believe he ever built any castles in the air on the strength of his own problematical prospects, or coveted the fair inheritance which accident might any day have made his. I cannot, of course, stoop to solicit a favour from the present Ministry, but I am gratified to hear that there is a prospect of his being put in command of a finer ship than that tiny gunboat, the Miriam—Murray—what was it?"

"The 'Midge,' papa," answered Nellie, blushing afresh, the instant her correction had been uttered, lest she should have

drawn attention to the tenacity of her
memory in all that related to the young
naval commander. But Sir Peregrine was
not in the habit of observing blushes, or of
drawing inferences from trivial circumstances such as he would have held a
change of colour on the part of his younger
daughter to be; while Adeline seemed quite
unconscious of her sister's artless agitation,
which was not, however, lost on Darrell's
quick eyes. One peculiarity there was, as
if tacitly established, in that uncongenial
family circle. Miss Conyers seldom looked
at Darrell, and still more rarely spoke to
him; while the boy scarcely ever addressed
a word to the kinswoman who from the
first had shown so marked an aversion to
him. Once already during the meal, the
tacit rule just mentioned had been deviated
from. When Darrell corroborated what the
younger of his two aunts had said, as to the
sudden noise caused by the clapping of a
door, the boy had looked steadily, not at
Nellie, but at Adeline, who had borne the

look with unruffled composure. And now, when her younger sister made mention of the real name of the gunboat lately the floating home of the coming cousin, Miss Conyers glanced, not at Nellie, but at the boy, as if to see whether he noted the signs of confusion which the speaker's face might have betrayed. But Darrell's bright, steady gaze remained quite careless, and his bearing unconstrained.

"I am sure I shall like him—this cousin of mine that I never saw—the captain," said the boy, in his usual outspoken manner. "I like sailors and the sea, and should have enjoyed a seafaring life myself, and to cruise to strange countries. Would you let me go for a voyage with Cousin Craven, if he should ask me, sir?" he continued, smiling. His grandfather had smiled, too, during the first portion of the boy's speech; and this was in itself no light proof of the high value which he placed upon his heir.

Sir Peregrine was one of those austere old disciplinarians who hold harsh theories as

to the fashion in which it behoves the
young to comport themselves before their
elders. The downright bluntness with
which a modern English boy contradicts
his father to his face, or pityingly sets his
mother right on things in general, was to
him positively offensive. In his heart, he
approved the Moslem code of etiquette,
which bids a son to stand, silent and
reverent, with downcast eyes and folded
arms before his sire ; nor had his dead son
Edmund, to whom he had been free-handed
enough in a pecuniary sense, ever at
Darrell's age been permitted to speak his
mind with the freedom which was allowed,
and even encouraged, in the case of the
grandson. But as he heard the last words,
Sir Peregrine's smile died away.

"It would never do," said Nellie, making
a desperate effort to speak with cheerful
unconcern, "for Darrell to be a sailor.
There would be too much risk then that
the old legend should——"

"Hush!" interrupted her father irritably;

"the Doom is not a subject, girl, to be lightly spoken of. Darrell's proper place, and his proper duties, are those of an English country gentleman. He will not find"—with a glance at the nice little heap of business letters which he had set apart—"that these are quite the sinecure which some suppose them to be. And that reminds me," added the baronet, as he gathered up his papers and rose from his seat, "that I have to ride out this morning—a long canter, too, across the hills, to Griffith's farm. I will order your pony to be saddled presently, Darrell, for I should like you to go with me?" This was said inquiringly, and his grandson's cheerful assent seemed to gratify the old man. "That is right, my boy," he said, laying his thin hand on Darrell's shoulder; "it is never too early to make yourself acquainted with the details of a large property, or to become known and respected by the tenantry. In an hour's time, I shall have answered the more pressing of these letters, and be ready to go."

"Pray," said Adeline languidly, "when did Captain Conyers mention his intention of arriving? You have not told us that, papa."

"True," said Sir Peregrine, turning back; "I forgot to say that he will be here to-morrow. You are mistress at the Towers, Adeline, and I shall be obliged to you to have whatever preparations are needed made without delay. You had better send for the housekeeper and give her her instructions at once." So saying, Sir Peregrine left the room, his dogs frisking around him, and the group dispersed. But long after Nellie and Darrell were gone, Adeline Conyers remained the sole occupant of the breakfast-room, standing, like a beautiful statue, her feet rooted to the ground, and her eyes fixed on vacancy, as if her fancy had the gift of peopling the empty air with some imagery unseen by others. She was one of those—they are but few—all whose attitudes are imbued with an unstudied grace: and as she thus stood, her out-

stretched arm and clenched hand added
to the strange impressiveness of the posture
which she had all unwittingly assumed.

For some moments Adeline stood silent,
pondering deeply, then in a low, deep tone
she broke the silence : — " I hate him ! "
she said passionately, " as on the first hour
when my eyes met his ; yet, mere child
though he be, I almost feel as if I feared
him too. Does he suspect me—he, a boy
whose mind should be busy with a boy's
sports and a boy's silly ambition to ape the
bearing of his elders ? No, the thought is
an idle one, and I fling it from me. Yet he
loves me, or I am shrewdly mistaken, no
whit better than I love him. A few years
more might make him a dangerous enemy,
this low-born brat, whose plebeian mother
infatuated my weak brother, and who is
soon—who knows how soon—to lord it over
the fair heritage that should of right belong
to myself, if not as heiress, then as wife to
the heir of Crag Towers. Yes, I hate him !
I could almost—may Heaven forgive the wild

thought!—pray night and morning that I might live to stand by yonder boy's couch, and see him dead!" She ceased speaking, and swept from the room in her stately beauty, as now the servants arrived to do their office, and sought her own apartments, the cruel words that she had spoken yet rankling at her heart. The time was to come when she should repent, ay, bitterly repent, with all the anguish of unavailing regret, that she had ever used them.

CHAPTER VI.

THE CAPTAIN'S VISIT.

BEFORE noon of the next day Captain
Craven Conyers, R.N., did arrive at Crag
Towers, and a fine young fellow he proved
to be, fully justifying the baronet's eulogy.
He was less of a Conyers, to look at, than
was usual among those of his stiff, unbend-
ing race, being of a healthy sunburnt complexion, with dark hair and eyes that very
well matched the bronzed tint which he
had brought back with him from sun-kissed
islands and summer seas far away. His
manner, too, was frankly sailor-like and
pleasant, and utterly free from the lazy
affectation of careless stolidity that marks
the swell of to-day from the dandy of
yesterday. Unless looks were sad mis-

leaders, those of the young commander gave true token of honour, sense, and courage, and did credit to the verdict of many a ward-room mess, and of many a quarter-deck, as to Craven's being " one of the best fellows " afloat beneath the Union Jack. He was in person slightly above the middle height, strong, active, and ever ready and willing to take his share in every athletic sport and out-door pastime. His description might have been summed up by saying that he was no bookworm and no genius, but a fine specimen of the manly and kindly young Englishman.

That he was well received under the roof beneath which his forefathers had dwelt, need scarcely be said. Sir Peregrine, who had often been sorely exercised in spirit by the faults and follies of his fashionable younger brother, had always shown favour to that brother's son, and made him heartily welcome to Crag Towers. Adeline's greeting was warmer, and her bearing perceptibly more gracious towards Captain Conyers than was ever the case when any other person, even high and mighty personages with strawberry-leaved coronets at their disposal in lawful wedlock, was concerned. But the young commander's lingering look, as he clasped his Cousin Nellie's hand, as though reluctant to release it, and the manner in which his eyes sought her face, whenever he fancied that such scrutiny would pass unobserved, told the old, old tale, that surely never will quite lose its freshness, in even a millennium of blue-spectacled Amazons of science. Will there ever dawn a day upon the world when the nightingale's song shall seem an unmeaning babble of bird-language, and the freshness of bud and flower, and tender greenery, lose its mute force of eloquence, and Love, his laughing eyes securely bandaged, his downy pinions clipped as closely as a convict's hair, be laid by the heels for aye, in the limbo to which have been consigned so many of the old-world beliefs and dreams? That dreary time may come, when love and lovers may be improved off the surface of the earth like the Red Indian; but, to judge by Nellie's trembling fingers as they felt, and perhaps returned, the pressure of the young sailor's hand, to judge, too, by the unbidden blush that suffused her rounded cheek, she, at any rate, was no convert to the dry tenets of the strong-minded sisterhood.

"And this, of course," said the captain, turning with extended hand toward the one member of the family group whom he now saw for the first time, "is my stranger-cousin, Darrell; not to be a stranger very long, I hope."

The boy met his kinsman with a smile as radiant as Craven's own. "I have heard of you more than once," he said readily; "and I was saying only yesterday that I was sure I should like you. I am more sure of it now."

Nothing, if speech-making be permissible in these undemonstrative times of ours, could be in better taste than this little utterance, yet, Craven scarcely knew why, the words produced somewhat of a chilling effect on the spirits of him to whom they were addressed. The captain was precisely one of those gay and gallant young men whom boys regard as heroes, in virtue of their pluck and muscles, and he had been popular with scores of Darrell's contemporaries, but the lad's very coolness disconcerted him. He would have been better pleased with his youthful cousin had he shown a little more of that ingenuous embarrassment and bashfulness which are so customary at his age, and privately set down the young heir as an insufferable prig and probably milksop. " If he behaves like this at thirteen "—such was Craven's mental reflection — " he will deserve to be an Under-Secretary of State at the very least, or a Junior Lord, before he is three-and-twenty. I'd rather not have to deal with him concerning dockyard business, I know that, when he shall have cut his official eye-teeth."

So here was a second person who had not, at first sight, taken a fancy to Darrell Conyers.

Then the gong sounded for lunch, and at that meal old Sir Peregrine was unusually chatty, having temporarily thawed, as it were, the icy envelope of taciturn reserve which habitually excluded him from easy conversational intercourse with others. He really had a good opinion of his nephew, and the more so, perhaps, because he was the only relative, beyond the limits of his own household, with whom he could be said to be on terms of friendly intimacy. His affection for his sister-in-law, Mrs. Craven Conyers, was of a very lukewarm order. Substantial proofs of his goodwill he had given without stint in those long-past days when Mrs. Craven's circumstances were prone to become uncomfortable in consequence of her colonel's amiable weakness for spending his wife's dividends twice over—in anticipation, and in reality; but there had never been much of sympathy between him and the worldly woman who had married his brother. Still, he had a sort of respect for Mrs. Conyers, of Paris, her tact and cleverness, and the high social consideration which she enjoyed. "I hope," he said very graciously, during a pause in the conversation, "that my sister is as well and charming as ever, and enjoying herself as usual?"

"Thanks; I believe so," answered the visitor, with a laugh. "The dear old lady gave me little or no rest, I know, while I was staying with her in the Rue Rococo, and insisted on dragging me, night after night, to embassy balls, and Venetian fêtes, and evening receptions, the *Italiens*, and the ministers' hotels. But I didn't like it. My French, I am afraid, was always of the lamest, so that I missed the point of the stories, and the pith of the gossip; and as for the petty jealousies and ambitions of the foreign residents, they amused me at first, but I soon grew to find them tiresome. It is wonderful at how low a rate nine-tenths of the sojourners in Paris, those of Anglo-Saxon stock, at all events, estimate one another, in comparison with any count or baron who may be a billiard-marker in masquerade for aught one can tell. How many Russians, Poles, Spaniards, do you know? and how few English or Americans? seemed to be the Shibboleth which my good mother's allies were perpetually propounding for the edification of a new comer amongst them. I was dreadfully weary of the whole thing, but perhaps that is because I am incorrigibly a John Bull."

Thus the young sailor rattled on, with a fluent volubility that was scarcely customary with him. He was quite right in describing himself as thoroughly an Englishman; and if there be one national characteristic of our race it is a tendency to be rather weighty than diffuse of speech, and to shun that rapid flow of winged words which is as natural to our Irish fellow-subjects as it is to Italians or Frenchmen. But Captain Conyers had a guilty consciousness that his eyes had met those of his younger cousin, and had been detected in so doing; and his desire was to cover Nellie's confusion, and to prove his own perfect self-possession by the smartness of his sallies. He did Sir Peregrine, however, something more than justice on the score of perspicacity. The baronet, even for a British father, was remarkably unsuspicious of any unauthorised sentiments which might be entertained towards his daughters. That both would one day marry and, in the conventional sense of the term, marry well, he regarded as the merest matter of course. Although no matchmaker, he felt tolerably confident that Adeline's beauty would win the reward of a rich and titled husband; while if even the phantom of Nellie's future mate flitted indistinctly before his mental vision, it assumed no shape less substantial than that of an estated gentleman, D.L. and J.P. of his county, and probably a good deal older than his bride. As for Craven, he was summarily classed among the many cadets of ancient families of whom it is declared, by their wealthier kinsfolk, that they "cannot afford" to marry, unless indeed they have the sense and luck to secure a well-dowered widow.

But although Sir Peregrine had no suspicions to discern, he had prejudices which were in some degree propitiated by the young commander's criticism on Lutetian life as he saw it, and the old man nodded his head with perfect contentment as his nephew concluded.

"Quite right," he said, "and very true. It is a frivolous, feverish, unreal existence altogether, and I do not wonder that you grew tired of it. No place, after all, like old England, though to be sure I had some French friends in the Faubourg St. Germain —I am speaking of forty years ago—who deserved the high opinion I had of them : excellent people in every relation of life."

And again he nodded, as his memory recalled the images of snuffy old dukes who wore brown coats and quoted Horace ; and of blameless marquises who knew no excite-

ment greater than a Lenten sermon, or a
quiet game at tric-trac with some silver-
haired abbé with a Breton surname and
shining shoe-buckles.

"I like Paris," said Adeline decisively.
"You did not stay there long enough,
cousin, to give the place or the society a
fair trial, I am afraid. Foreigners, you
know, have sometimes the bad taste not to
enjoy themselves in London."

"Very likely," answered the captain, with
a good-humoured smile; "and very likely,
too, I did not bring to the Rue Rococo a
mind quite free from bias. I never enjoyed,
as a boy, I well remember, any holidays so
well as those I spent in England, and was
ungrateful enough to be wretched among
the polished floors and silk hangings of the
worthy folks, my mother's friends, who
patted me on the cheek and tried to feed
me with bonbons. I suspect that every one
likes what suits him the best, and that our
strictures merely mean that we are not
adapted for the particular ways and habits

which we condemn. Of one thing I am
sure, and that is that I am heartily glad to
find myself again at Crag Towers. The dear
old place is looking charmingly well."

The conversation then turned on the old
mansion, its demesne, and its neighbourhood, of which there was much to ask and
to tell. Births, deaths, and marriages had
to be chronicled and commented upon, and
then the estate itself was a topic almost
inexhaustible. There does indeed seem to
be something in the possession of land, in
large or small quantities, which furnishes
an unfailing subject of engrossing interest
to the owner. No sailor can talk of his
ship, no dean of his cathedral, no don of
his college, with quite the sense of solid
enjoyment with which your territorial magnate rides the hobby of his broad acres and
their management. Again, a great talker,
and still more, a silent man who has for
once in a way been beguiled into loquacity,
is almost sure to rise from table with a
considerable respect for the conversational

powers of the brilliant listener to whom his remarks have been addressed. Nor is it surprising that, when the meal was over, Sir Peregrine, who had taken the lion's share of what was said concerning his lands and beeves, estimated his nephew Craven as most capital company.

In the course of the afternoon, as he renewed his acquaintance with the house and grounds, with which, as a juvenile guest, he had once been fairly familiar, the captain saw cause to change his opinion as to the heir's disposition. The party had strayed along a meadow-path that led through the pleasant orchards and crofts bordering on the spreading park, when Darrell, who had left the house a little later than the rest, appeared near the pheasantry, the only approach to which was by a stile. A high, hog-backed, old-fashioned stile it was, of the stamp that has occasioned many an ugly fall and broken collar-bone with the foxhounds. Captain Conyers, who looked on Darrell as a sucking pedant, fully expected to see him crawl over this impediment in the slow and bear-like method which we often remark in studious youth. But, to his surprise, and without apparent effort, the boy cleared it like a bird.

" You must have been well used to rowing to handle an oar like that ! " said Craven, when, later in the day, they rowed among the islets of the lake; and it was from the underkeeper that he learned in how brief a time Darrell had acquired such mastery of the sculls : while the unanimous verdict of the stable-yard was that the future lord of Crag Towers had in him the " making " of such a horseman as would do credit to the shire.

" It's very odd," said Craven to himself, as he dressed for dinner ; " but it really does seem as if Miss Conyers yonder had a dislike, and a strong one, to the boy. It's impossible not to remark it; and, indeed, I was not at first very much prepossessed in his favour. I had rather give a wide berth to your Pic de Mirandolas and infant pro-

digies, but this youngster wins upon me
somehow."

And such, in effect, was the general im-
pression which Darrell produced on those
with whom he came in contact—the one
notable exception being that of Sir Peregrine's eldest daughter, whose feelings towards him were even more bitter than she
ventured to own to herself. But the young
sailor had a more attractive subject for his
meditations than any boy, howsoever bright
and gifted, could be. He thought Nellie
Conyers to be looking even prettier than he
had pictured her to himself, and yet he had
treasured up her image in his heart of
hearts as he cruised over many a weary
league of sea, and lay for many a day at
anchor off the low blue coasts, or within
the white coral reefs of the Atolls, with the
heavy surf breaking in thunder on the gird-
ling barrier that fenced the smooth water
from the rollers beyond, and with the palm-
trees and thatched huts dotting the shore
line. Yes, she was pretty, sweet, and true,

and pure, and she cared for him—at least a little—or so he fancied: and he was glad to be where he could see her every day, and breathe the same air, and be, for the time being at any rate, mixed up with her life. And yet there was always present with him the uneasy recollection that he would be, in the eyes of the world and those of Nellie's father, no proper mate for a daughter of Sir Peregrine's.

"How queer that seems!" the young man muttered to himself as he threw a glance out of the window near him, and which overlooked the stately deer park and the ornamental lake. "How queer that seems, considering that the governor was born here, just as Sir Peregrine was, and in their nursery days and school time they were both on an equality. Ah! well, I suppose it's all right, and so forth—and I've often heard old gentlemen prove the law of primogeniture to be a great blessing to us here in England, and that sort of thing. How different would have been my position, in the baronet's eyes, as an eligible son-in-law, had poor Edmund left no son to succeed to the entailed estates! If this young Darrell——" He paused, reddening to the temples, although alone, at the idea that he had been perilously near to the expression of an unworthy sentiment. "I don't grudge the boy his good luck, or his birthright," he said, as if apologizing to some invisible audience; and, after all, I suspect he will make a far better master of Crag Towers than I should ever have done. But if my poor father had had his share of all these fat acres—to be sure," he added, with a laugh and a sigh, "he would have been certain to have spent it, so things are just as well as they are." And so saying, he dismissed the subject, for his was a breast too honest to harbour envy.

The evening passed away pleasantly enough. There was music, and there was conversation, and even a turn or two of the waltz. It was Nellie with whom the captain danced, while Adeline obligingly took her seat at the piano. Nellie played but did not sing. Adeline sang and played, and that with a rare merit that by far surpassed the modest performance of her sister. Her voice was wonderfully well modulated, sweet, and flexible; now ringing through the large room like the call of a clarion, now whispering as the summer wind whispers among the reeds of a river. She had been admirably well taught, and was mistress of every art by which the effect of a song can be enhanced; but on that evening, somewhat to Nellie's surprise, she discarded her favourite pieces, which●were operatic gems, and gave the preference to simple and touching English ballads, to which she imparted a pathos which drew Craven Conyers, he hardly knew how, close to the instrument at which Adeline had placed herself.

"She is very beautiful—Adeline—after all!" Thus ran his thoughts as he watched her, hearkening the while to the dying fall of her excellently-managed voice, and looking on her with deserved admiration for her exquisite loveliness. What a silver-clear voice was hers, too, and what quiet grace there was in every attitude! Her dress, too, skilfully selected, became her well, and the very flashing of her bracelet, as her deft fingers ran over the ivory keys, served to call attention to the rounded whiteness of an arm that was perfect in its proportions. It was not her fault, surely, that the effect of some minutes' conversation with her and contemplation of her seemed to be that of making poor Nellie's pretty face look almost homely, and her simple talk sound trite and dull. It is, indeed, a world-old trick, that fashion which beautiful sisters have occasionally the cruelty to practise, of dazzling and misguiding the admirers of those who are less beautiful. Who has not seen Kate "cutting down" poor bashful Lucy before the bewildered eyes of her curate; or Florence temporarily depriving Jane of the allegiance of him whom irreverent housemaids describe as "the young man she keeps company with ? " These tactics, however, are as transparent as they are heartless, and succeed better in cubhood than with men who have had some larger share of worldly experience. Miss Conyers was by far too proud openly to enter the lists with her sister, or to make a parade of her accomplishments for her mortification. On the contrary, nothing could exceed the gentleness of her manner to Nellie, or her evident consideration for her younger sister's welfare. There was a graceful, loving patronage in her treatment of her for whom Craven's preference had from the first been obvious, which became her well, and there was no sign of her usual imperiousness in speech or deportment.

So it came about, that as the evening progressed, Nellie grew to be more and more silent, and seemed, as it were, to shrink into herself, and to yield to her brilliant competitor the place which the latter seemed so unwilling to claim. Nellie's sunshiny nature was for the time over-

clouded by an uneasy sense of wrong.
Jealousy seldom allows any girl to appear
at her best, being but a poor passion after
all; and yet, although it would not be
strictly true that Nellie was jealous of her
sister, she entertained an uncomfortable feeling as regarded Adeline's conduct, specious
though it were. Perhaps there is something unerring in the instinct by which one
woman knows when another would play her
false, would jockey her, so to speak, off
the course matrimonial; and slow as the
younger Miss Conyers was to think evil,
she could not be satisfied. There was
generally no medium in Adeline's deportment. Where she did not care to please
she was brusque, haughty, and hostile; but
when it seemed worth her while she had a
method of demanding homage that rarely
failed of its effect. Now she was gentle,
sympathetic, almost timid, and the attention
was by no means agreeable to Nellie as she
saw, or thought she saw, Craven becoming
gradually entangled in the snares of the too

lovely enchantress. It would have been balm to her spirit, however, had she known how unshaken was the young man's loyal love for herself. That he should admire Adeline was inevitable, but it was as something strange and beautiful that he regarded her, worthy of attention certainly, but by no means to be brought into comparison with her on whom his heart was set.

That night Craven Conyers had a singular dream. His sleeping eyes beheld a giddy rock that overlooked the stormy sea, and on its edge, robed in glistening, gauzy tissue, harp in hand, and flower-crowned, was a siren that sat and sang, and drew him towards her, his feet appearing to advance in despite of his own will. And the siren's lustrous eyes, and flaxen hair, and tempting beauty, were strangely like to those of Adeline, and she waved her white arms, and wreathed them, beckoning. Then suddenly the expression of her fair features changed to one of hate and fury, as another form appeared, with upturned face, as its owner strove to climb the precipice, and the face was that of Darrell Conyers, not now full of buoyant life, but blanched and haggard with a great terror. Then came a confused memory of a hasty struggle, and then a piercing shriek, and both figures were gone, and the rock-edge in the moonlight was empty and bare; and Craven awoke, with throbbing heart and heated brow, to be glad that it was a dream.

in wrong. It was not only in looks that these delighted village patriarchs recognized a resemblance between the baronet that was to be and the belted heroes of the legends of the hamlet. They whispered to one another, with somewhat of gleeful reverence, that "the young master had a will of his own, ay, and a temper too," and thus hailed him as a worthy chip of the tough old Conyers' block. That the boy knew his own mind, and was fully alive to the nature of his own position, was indeed pretty plain. Nor was it less clear that he meant others to remember it. But it was not often that Sir Peregrine's grandson had any need for angry self-assertion. The peculiarly frank fearlessness of his speech, the steadiness of his bright gaze, and his entire freedom from affectation or sheepishness, rendered it extremely difficult for any one to try experiments on his patience or his credulity. He had the gift, in which kings and princes have often been lacking, and which is the appanage of no station, of winning the respect of those whom he encountered on his way through life. It became the general opinion of the country side that when Master Darrell should grow to be a man, whoever withstood or quarrelled with him would very probably be in the wrong, and more surely still would get the worst of the collision.

But it was not only because, beneath a smooth exterior, he was credited with possessing much of the fierce spirit which had distinguished his race, that Darrell was liked even by those who cherished no great affection for the class to which he belonged or for the name he bore. Wherever he went a malcontent was conciliated or a partisan won, thanks to some indefinable charm of manner which it was all but impossible to resist. The women raved about his good looks ; the men were, if less enthusiastic, at any rate impressed by the sight of that bold, bright face that suggested sunshine breaking in upon dark places, as its owner went amongst the slow-speaking hinds who

tilled the soil. Those who had much to
say, the mouthpieces of new ideas, were
complimented by so intelligent a listener,
and often predicted what an improving
landlord and genial magistrate they should
have one day in Sir Darrell Conyers. There
are always those who revel in anticipation
of the golden age to be commenced when
the young prince comes to his own, and
who are often disappointed at discovering
what a commonplace king the dauphin
makes after all. Sundry persons who had
private ends to serve looked to Darrell as
their destined instrument; while others,
with the vague aspiration after change
which is inherent in human nature, per-
sisted in regarding the boy as a sort of
parochial Haroun Alraschid who would go
about reducing rents, giving allotments,
perquisites, and rights of pannage, turbary,
and fishery, and somehow or other making
everybody on the estate happy and con-
tented.

There were other neighbours whose

higher social station gave weight to the
encomiums which they uttered, and whose
approval of the embryo owner of Crag
Towers was as balm to Sir Peregrine's
sensitive ears. The noble father of that
juvenile Lord Fitzharry, whose address we
have heard Nellie contrast with that of
Darrell, and Sir Hugh, sire of "the Neville
boys," to whom at the same time allusion
was made, were as hearty in the boy's praise
as were the family at the rectory, or red-
faced Mr. Buckthorne, M. F. H. of the
Wyeside hunt, into whose good graces the
boy may be said to have not crept, but
galloped, since it was his rapid proficiency
in the equestrian art which won over the
bluff old foxhunter. "Master Darrell," so
said his admirers of the stable-yard over
their beer, "must have been born booted
and spurred—he do so take to it, he do."
And it was true that, fast as was the young
heir's progress in every physical accom-
plishment, it was in the saddle that he
seemed to be the most completely at home.

The very grooms who taught him to ride stared at the unwonted promptitude with which their pupil profited by their lessons; while as for that part of an instructor's duty which consists in the encouragement of a neophyte, it seemed a sinecure. "Don't be over venturesome, pray, sir!" was a warning that had many a time and oft to be offered to the too daring tyro; and it was unanimously averred that if any boy in the county had his heart in the right place, that youthful personage was certainly Sir Peregrine's grandson.

That Sir Peregrine himself should come to be very fond and proud of the boy was but natural. We must be singularly un-lucky if we are not prodigies in the eyes of our grandfathers, and the baronet had an unusually good excuse for the high value which he set on his successor in the title. We all of us measure the moral and mental stature of those who are near and dear to us by the help of that invisible standard which we call public opinion. And then

Sir Peregrine had been harsh—possibly, his conscience whispered, unjust—to one who was gone beyond the reach of earthly atonement, and the memory of Edmund Conyers pleaded eloquently on behalf of his surviving son. He could not steel himself against this new candidate for his paternal love; and though he had often been stern, sometimes capricious, in his dealings with his own offspring, he would have done very much to avoid the addressing of even a word of reproof to young Darrell. To all these reasons for the influence which the boy was gradually gaining over his grandfather may be added another. The stronger spirit never can fail to impress the weaker, nor can all the artificial inequalities of social life efface this fact, proved by hourly experience. Are there no servants who rule a weak mistress with a rod of iron?—no awful head-gardeners and plausible stud-grooms, of whom poor Crœsus, for all his bank balance and his M.P.ship, stands in dread?—no monarchs who feel uncomfortable in their

royal shoes when the great minister comes
frowningly to take audience of his august
master? There were moments when the
old man, dimly conscious of the sort of
ascendency which this child was establish-
ing over his senior, grew almost angry at
the thought of it; but he might as well
have tried to interfere with the earth's
rotation as to prevent himself from attach-
ing more importance to Darrell's words
and wishes than his severe theories allowed.
It was not merely that the boy was brave
and clever and quick to learn. Sir Peregrine regarded courage as merely an integral
part of a gentleman's nature, and had somewhat of that half-reasoning antipathy to
intellect, as a sort of wild elephant or
explosive compound that might do mischief one day, which we often find among
those who have much to lose, and nothing
to gain, by change.

What really, in Darrell Conyers, extorted
Sir Peregrine's unspoken admiration was
the peculiar dauntlessness of his speech

and bearing. A shy, silent man is apt to
envy assurance and a ready wit, as a negro
envies a white skin. And Sir Peregrine
had all his life long been one of those
painful persons who weigh their words, and
think of their dignity before uttering each
carefully-chosen sentence. Those who have
this unfortunate peculiarity are never, as a
matter of fact, popular; and the baronet's
pride also was of that unsocial kind that
turns inwards, not of the sort that sets off,
like the gold around a jewel, every gift of
the possessor, by the simple process of
inspiring confidence. Darrell's pride, if he
had any pride, was of the positive, not the
negative variety. Imperious he might be
on occasion, but he never showed signs of
that morose self-appreciation which seems
to enwrap its possessor as a shell does an
oyster.

Darrell was at an age when the zest of
life is very keen; and to all appearance he
enjoyed the plenteous shower of the world's
good things that had fallen to his share, and

was as blithe and light of heart as any boy
of his years. But real happiness is scarcely
consistent with sustained and anxious
efforts, whether the object be to acquire
wealth or to court popularity. And if Darrell Conyers did not strive, and scheme,
and practise the arts of a candidate laying
siege to a constituency, then it must be
admitted that a marvellous series of coin-
cidences provided for his being, nine times
out of ten, in the right place, and doing
and saying precisely what was most likely
to raise him in the estimation of those with
whom he came in contact. Had he been a
man and not a boy, people might have come
to speculate on "Master Darrell's" apparent
eagerness to be surrounded by well-wishers
of every degree, and to wonder why he
seemed so desirous to conciliate those whose
goodwill could in very few conceivable circumstances stand him in good stead. But
youth is proverbially the season for guileless
mirth, and a boy is no more likely to be suspected of any design deeper than to crop the

pleasure of the passing moment, than if he were a sort of human butterfly. Now and again, indeed, there would be times when a sudden and singular change of mood came over the bright nature of Sir Peregrine's grandson; and a strange air of weariness and lassitude would replace the boy's sunny looks, and for a few minutes he would grow silent, almost sullen, and if speaking at all would reply in such enigmatical fashion as puzzled the bystanders. Never for long, however; and it was always remarked that after one of these temporary eclipses, Darrell's gay, bold spirit shone out more brilliantly than before. Nor were these transient fits of half-cynical depression ever known to occur when Miss Conyers was present, for before her the young heir always appeared at his best, as if her evident aversion acted as a stimulant to his powers of pleasing.

Meanwhile Captain Conyers continued to be a resident beneath Sir Peregrine's roof, and was on the best of terms with every

member of the household. He had quickly
conquered his early prejudice against the
boy, and in fact his generous nature caused
him to be foremost in commending Darrell's
many and undoubted merits, the rather that
it was Sir Peregrine's grandson who stood
between himself and the rich inheritance
which would otherwise have one day de-
volved upon him.

"A fine lad!" he would say laughingly,
in good-humoured protest against Adeline's
frequent sneers—"a fine lad, and just the
one to make his way in the world, if Fortune had not been kind enough to provide
him with so soft a nest without the trouble
of feathering it. I wish, cousin, that I
could see you and him better friends. I
am sure he bears you no ill-will, so the
alteration would be a one-sided affair after
all."

"We are fire and water!" flashed out
Adeline, with the usual glitter in her eyes
and the usual curl on her haughty lip; "and
when fire and water swear a friendship,

Darrell and I shall agree. No ill-will on his part! You believe that, I know, since you say it. You are a man and a sailor, cousin, and do not look for sunken rocks and hidden shoals anywhere but at sea. Excuse a woman for trusting more to her own powers of perception, where social matters are concerned, than to yours. Darrell is as deep and as secret as the grave, but he cannot mislead me as to the return he would make me, if he could, for the feelings which I have never cared to conceal."

" I still think you are wrong," said Craven smiling, " and I am afraid you have never forgiven your nephew the acci-dent of his parentage. If his mother had been one of the Nevilles, now, or belonged to any of the old families round us here, you would have seen him, I suspect, with very different eyes. It is not the poor boy's fault, remember, if his father did marry—imprudently."

Captain Craven Conyers, like many an-

other manly young fellow, had his own
opinion on the subject of those unions
which "society" condemns as unequal. Had
he been in love with a good girl of a grade
even inferior to that of Mark Meanwell's
sister, he would not have permitted all the
Grundies of Grundydom to bar his way to
the hymeneal altar. But as it so happened
that the young lady to whom he was attached was above his reach, the temptation
to outrage the canons of Belgravian etiquette
by marrying outside the pale was lacking,
nor did he care to enter into a probably
useless argument in defence of Edmund's
rash choice. Hence his use of the mildly
ambiguous term "imprudent," when speaking to Miss Conyers on the sore subject
of her brother's marriage ; and the honest
sailor reddened at his own diplomatism as
he uttered the phrase. Adeline did not
answer, save by a bitter little laugh, and
Craven turned away baffled, feeling that
his advocacy of Darrell was hopeless, unless
length of time could gradually overcome

the deeply-rooted prejudice which Sir Peregrine's eldest daughter entertained against the universal favourite.

The young commander had other matters to occupy his thoughts than Adeline's aversion, however unreasonable that might be, to her nephew Darrell. Before he arrived at Crag Towers he would have declared it to be impossible that he should become more deeply in love with Nellie than he already was. But he had underrated the powerful influence of propinquity to a beloved object, and had presently to recognize the truth that, were he bound to renounce for ever the hope of one day converting his sweet cousin into his wife, he could no longer confront the world with the same lightsome heart and serene brow as formerly. There was a magic in Nellie's company, in breathing the same air, in being thrown daily and hourly into her society, which was in some respects very pleasant, but carried with it its sting to counterbalance the honey. A few quickly passing days or weeks, and he must go. And then, when once the dear face could no longer be seen, he should feel himself alone indeed, should realize fully, bitterly the loneliness of his position. And his was not a deprivation which the world would pity or even fathom. A young man in his position had socially no matrimonial status. And Craven groaned as he acknowledged that his hopes would be reckoned as presumption, even by tolerably good-natured critics, and that there was no father of marriageable daughters in all England less likely to smile upon his suit than was Sir Peregrine.

Nellie, on the other hand, was happy. Women who know that they are loved have a power of living in the present which is denied to men. The restless masculine mind is always looking forward, always craving for some boon which the future has in store, while a girl can be as calmly and contentedly joyous in the company of her plighted lover as if the poet's wild conceit had been fulfilled, and the troublesome conditions of time and space no longer existed. Craven had not told his pretty cousin that he cared for her— had not told her so, that is to say, in plain terms such as necessitate a reference to papa or the summoning of a family council to make or mar the match. Yet she was as well aware of the fact as if it had been posted on the walls, in the biggest and blackest of type at the billsticker's command. She knew, too, that her fears had been groundless as to the probability of Adeline's being able to supplant her in Craven's heart by virtue of her superior beauty and talents.

Nellie could not fail to note that her brilliant elder sister had striven to rob her of her lover, but she almost forgave Adeline the fruitless attempt, for the simple reason that it was fruitless. Even the gentlest do not always dislike a struggle for a suitor's affections when the contest ends satisfactorily. It was clear that Adeline, when calling to her aid those dangerous fascina-

tions which belonged to her, could do no
more than engage Craven's attention, not
touch his heart; and this delicious knowledge
it was that made the younger Miss Conyers
enjoy the hours spent with her sailor-cousin
without being saddened by the prospect of
the future. When he should go away, then
indeed she should be badly off, living as it
were on the memory of a dream: but to this
contingency she resolutely closed her eyes.
He was at Crag Towers now, at any rate,
and he loved her, and was true to her, like a
faithful knight whom the wiles of an enchantress could not win away from the lady
whose colours he wore; and she would be
happy now, let what would occur to throw a
gloom over to-morrow.

That is a very delightful stage on the
royal road—ever new, though so old that
the earlier feet that trod it are forgotten
dust—along which Love leads us; the stage,
that is to say, when the soft secret is
mutually betrayed at each instant, yet when
no direct proposal or avowal has been made.

That is the time for pretty trifling, for transparent stratagems and mysteries that deceive nobody, for hints and little jests, and stolen glances, and gentle murmurs of reproach, so gentle that each modulated accent seems a caress. Cupid is forging and fitting on the golden chains, be sure; but as yet the pressure of the fairy fetters is so light as to be almost unfelt. There is a sweet sense of an existing tie, and yet a feeling as if the unacknowledged link were so fragile that it must be spared all strain and pressure. Each of the persons principally concerned is somewhat in the position of Fortunatus, with the magic purse safe in his pocket, but as yet delaying to extract the unfailing supply of gold coins; of a king, perhaps, who walks in poor disguise, undetected, among his swarming people, but who knows he has but to pronounce a word, to hold aloft a flashing signet ring, to call around him guards and courtiers and all the pomp of eastern royalty.

Such was the state of affairs as Craven

and Nellie walked together through the
darkling shrubbery, late in the afternoon of
the day on which the former had put in his
apologetic plea with Miss Conyers on the
subject of her too evident antipathy to
Darrell. There was a grey haze over-
spreading the sky; the white clouds that
rolled along before the breeze had acquired
a tint of copper, the foreteller of a storm,
and the weather was hot and oppressive;
while over the Welsh mountains, to the
westward, brooded a black cloud-bank like
an adamantine wall. But they two recked
little of these meteorological warnings, until
a low muttering growl of distant thunder was
followed by the descent of a few broad drops
of rain, heavy and flat, that rattled among
the leaves. Then, of course, it suggested
itself to Craven that Nellie would get wet;
and Nellie, equally of course, was certain
that the storm "would come to nothing,"
and so commenced one of those pleasant
prattling arguments so frequent with those
who stand towards one another in that

agreeable relation of life which precedes betrothal. But the storm took Craven's side in the discussion, and the young man had to wrap his pretty cousin's light shawl closely around her, and to hurry her off towards the house, while the beating rain fell in sheets, and the red flashes, and the deep roar of the thunder, told of the quick approach of the tempest.

When once the lovers were out of sight, from a path parallel to that which they had pursued in quitting the shrubbery there emerged the graceful form and handsome, jealous face of Adeline Conyers. She was bareheaded, and there was something characteristic in the utter indifference with which she stood beneath a huge cedar, while the rain lashed her, and the dazzling radiance of the lightning flashed before her steady eyes. For some minutes she thus stood, heedless of the fact that her garments were drenched, and her hair draggled with wet, gazing at the spot where the lovers had last been seen.

"So, so," she said softly; "it is as I thought; the game is not won yet, sister of mine." And without another word she walked on to the house.

CHAPTER VIII.

AT THE COMMODORE'S COTTAGE.

" WILL you walk with me to-day just across the park ? " inquired Craven, as he found himself, in company with his two cousins, on the smooth croquet lawn, studded with massive clumps of rhododendron, that was overlooked by the Gothic windows of Sir Peregrine's library : " I mean," added the young man, " as far as Captain Killick's. I had to thank the old man for many a kindness in my midshipman days, and he would never forgive it if I appeared to neglect him now. We should be sure to find him at this hour."

The question was put with apparent impartiality to both or either of the young ladies addressed, but Adeline it was who

took it upon herself to reply. "I cannot
spare the time, unfortunately," she made
answer, "since I was rash enough to
mention, in Lady Neville's hearing, those
wonderful new flowers that Macfarlane has
got from a correspondent of his in Brazil, or
Bermuda, I am not sure which. The excellent woman is, as you know, floriculturally
mad, and I was obliged to pledge myself to
be at home and ready to introduce her to
the novel importations. I think I see the
carriage now coming up the avenue; and
unless you and Nellie want to be caught
and caged in the conservatory to listen to
botanical Latin, you will take the path by
the lake, and catch the dear old captain
before he sallies forth for his daily stroll."

The suggestion was a good-natured one, to
all appearance, and as such Craven received
it. Adeline Conyers, however, looked after
the young people as they departed, with a
very dubious expression on her cold, fair
face. Her appointment with Lady Neville
was real enough, but she would have thrown

over her floral ladyship with few scruples,
had the young sailor invited her personally
to be the companion of his walk. As it was,
no one was better aware of the truth that
three compose but an awkwardly constituted
company, or was less disposed to accept the
humble part of gooseberry-picker than was
Miss Conyers, and of this Nellie divined
something as her sister uttered her specious
little speech. But still she felt half grateful
to Adeline, whatsoever were her motives,
for thus securing her the pleasant stroll
among the glades, at Craven's side. It was
a day of brilliant beauty; the hot morning
sun had dried the paths and kissed away
from fern and grass blade every drop of
moisture which the heavy rain of yesterday
evening had left behind. The birds were
singing with a joyful shrillness very different
from the twitter of alarm with which but
yesterday they had sought refuge from the
crashing storm, and the leaves and turf
merely looked the more freshly green for the
recent elemental war.

On the lovers went, therefore, past the
the lake, with its tall reed banks and sedgy
shores, beloved by the silver swans; past the
giant trees that had grown up in that fair
pleasaunce of which they appeared to be the
colossal guardians, untouched by the sacri-
legious axe of the woodman; past dells, at
the bottom of which lurked tiny black pools
where the deer stooped their antlered heads
to drink; past banks where a colony of
rabbits sported, while scores of half-tame
pheasants exhibited their gorgeous plumage
and well-fed plumpness on the verge of the
pine copse a little higher up. Every leaflet,
each wild flower, every frond of the fern,
assumed a rarer beauty for them, than
would have been visible to common
observers. They walked lingeringly, therefore, as if in no hurry to pass the frontiers
of fairyland and issue out once more into
the gross work-a-day world that lay beyond.
So it befell that, although the walk to
Captain Killick's place of abode was not a
very long one, a good deal of time was
consumed in getting there.

It was a pretty cottage, that of the old naval officer, and prettily situated close to a side gate opening into the park, so that the occupant of the small house could overlook, through the parcel-gilt ironwork, the stately demesne that belonged to the castle beyond the lake. But Captain Killick, more commonly known in the village as Commodore Killick, was much more proud of gazing at the beauties contained within his own boundaries than of fancying himself the lord of those swelling uplands and timbered glades that appertained to his wealthier neighbour. It was a source of undying satisfaction to the old seaman that he lived on his own freehold property, and that, as he often said, every stick and stone about the little place was his. He was Sir Peregrine's very good friend, but he would not have liked to be Sir Peregrine's tenant. The great Conyers' estate girdled him in on every side like the possessions of the Marquis of Carabas encircling the petty heritage of some infinitesimal proprietor;

and the commodore's tiny domain was as
an island in the midst of lands the rents of
which were paid to the baronet's steward.
Yet of those four or five acres that lay
within the blossomed hedge, fragrant with
sweet briar and honeysuckle, the owner had
contrived to make a good deal. His lawn,
as he boasted, was a dead flat, on which the
croquet balls ran truer than on the spreading
velvet of the much larger lawn at Crag
Towers. He was immeasurably vain of pro-
ducing more monstrous strawberries, and
in greater variety, than the great Macfarlane
himself, the learned and high-salaried head-
gardener at the Castle, had done. In hot-
house flowers, indeed, the commodore made
no attempt to compete, but in roses he was
supreme; and he loved to train his rose
trees into floral umbrellas, crosses, pyramids,
and other fantastic and unexpected shapes,
and to devise surprises in the way of bud
and petal.

The commodore's ambition was by no
means limited to roses and strawberries.

There might be but one cow to crop the
herbage of his little meadow, but what a cow!
the very model of a milker in shape, colour,
docility, and every bovine virtue known!
His pet pony was clever enough to have
deserved an engagement at Astley's; and
had the judicious peculiarity of allowing no
one to drive him, save the commodore
himself, being the most vigorous and
determined kicker that ever wore harness.
There was a fish-pond full of big tame carp
that knew their proprietor as well as they
knew the sound of the brass plate that was
daily beaten as their dinner bell, and would
accept biscuit from his hand in all the
nibbling serenity of complete confidence.
There were famous rabbits, and carrier
pigeons supposed to be able to find their
way back to their dovecote at the Lilacs
from any part of Western Europe. And
as for the fancy poultry! Captain Killick
scorned to waste his care on mere Cochins
and Brahmas and Crèvecœurs, accessible to
everybody. His miniature yard was stocked

with unheard-of breeds, the feathered
ancestors of which he had brought home
in various voyages on board the famous
frigates which he had long commanded,
and the praises of which he sang as Homer
chanted those of the spear-throwing heroes
of Hellas.

It is perhaps strange that Captain Killick,
being a man who rode so many hobbies at
once—and all whose geese, to use the homely
but forcible idiom of rural life, were swans—
should have been long numbered among
the most intimate friends · of the haughty
Conyers family, and should have been, as
he was, the person from whom Sir Peregrine
would take in good part what would have
given mortal offence if spoken by another.
But very proud men, and even very proud
kings, sometimes affect the society of bluff
boors, whose trenchant way of telling un-
palatable truths braces the nerves enervated
by sycophantic deference. And the commodore was no more a bluff boor than Sir
Peregrine was a king; being in fact the

nephew of an Irish earl, between whose
family and that of Conyers there was one
of those convenient links of far-off kins-
manship which can be ignored, repudiated,
eagerly claimed, or grudgingly admitted,
according to the relative social standing of
the remote cousins. He was, however, one
of those exceptional mortals who disdain
to bend the knee to the Baal of prosperity,
yet whose generous souls are free from a
taint of that envy which vitiates many a
stinging philippic against the great of the
earth. He saw Dives as he was, and was
by far too sturdy to abate a jot of the truth
by reason of the pomp and splendour that
environed him. But then he did not hate
the man, as some do, for the offence given
by his purple and fine linen.

The gate bell, the bronze handle of which
had been lawful spoil of war, carried off
from some Burmese joss-house by a British
boat's crew, and which, in the neighbourhood of London, would soon have found its
way to the emporium of some dealer in

marine stores, clanged forth its summons
at the touch of Craven's hand, and was
promptly answered by a grinning negro,
with crisp white curls, like so much silver
wool, topping a receding black forehead,
in the centre of which were indelibly impressed, in light blue, some intricate pagan
patterns of African tattooing. The negro
was old, but active and jaunty of aspect,
and very strongly built withal; for although
his stature was low, the spreading torso was
that of a sable Hercules, while more than
one white scar that seamed his swarthy
cheek contrasted oddly with the golden ear-
rings, the neat tie of the bright-coloured
cravat, and the showy watch chain, in the
extreme style of maritime dandyism, which
this remarkable serving-man wore. He was
clad in a glossy suit of shore-going clothes,
of good broad-cloth, but a few sizes too
large for him; and had a roll in his gait,
and a twinkle in his glowing eyes, which
forbade the most careless observer to class
him as a landsman.

"Servant, Massa Lieutenant—beg pardon, Cap'en Conyers!" said the negro, with a sea bow, and a sea scrape of the foot, while his glittering teeth, filed to a point, and as sound and sharp as when their owner had first been chained down in a slave barracoon on the Guinea coast, flashed forth an amicable recognition. "Servant, Miss Nellie!" and he bowed again, while his opal eyes expressed more, after their grotesque fashion, in the way of deferential friendliness, than European eyes ever do.

"How goes the world with you, Scipio?" said Craven smiling. "You don't look a day older than when you and I were shipmates aboard the old *Thunderbolt*, off Zanzibar, there."

"And a very mischievous young gentleman your honour was, always skylarking with the wildest of the young reefers in calm weather—ready 'nough, though, in a squall, or for service. You forget de boat work, Massa Craven, eh? and how we lost sight of ship; and two, tree day we row, row, under hot sun, short of water and provisions, looking out for dem slaver villains; you forget dat, sir?"

"Indeed I do not," answered the young commander; "nor how you received that ugly cut on the cheekbone, my good friend, in saving me from the stroke of an Arab's sabre, as we boarded the dhow. The turbaned rascal had disabled my right wrist, as it was, and was swinging back his lean brown arm for a fair slash at my neck, when you scrambled in between us, and let him have it with your tomahawk. But we must not spin these yarns before ladies," he added, seeing that Nellie had turned pale at the recital of this adventure. "Is the commodore at home, Scipio?"

"Massa Commodore in 'um state cabin, massa," answered the black briskly, and he forthwith led the way across the little entrance-hall, replete with infallible barometers, umbrella stands of quaint device,

and glass cases full of stuffed fish and birds
of tropic plumage; and opening an oaken
door, ceremoniously announced the visitors,
whom he now inducted into the presence
of the master of the house. The drawing-
room, never so called either by Scipio or
its owner, really did resemble a cabin, the
panelled walls being ingeniously fitted
with a profusion of lockers, while the look-
ing-glasses and pictures were by far less
conspicuous than were two star-shaped
trophies of arms, one of which consisted
simply of ship's muskets and pistols, cutlasses, boarding pikes, and tomahawks. The
other, however, was worthy of a more
prolonged inspection, being composed of
weapons the most various—swords, sabres,
scimitars, and daggers, straight or curved,
the kreeses and kliowangs of the Malay,
grouped with Turkish pistols, Moorish guns
and battle-axes, the barbed spear of the
savage, and the steel mace of the Sikh
warrior. Many of these weapons were
splendidly mounted in silver, ivory, and

even gold and precious stones, and they
were tastefully grouped around a handsome
shield, the burnished bosses on which had
once gratified the vanity of a Bornean
pirate chief. On the tables were knick-
knacks innumerable, in ivory, rhinoceros
horn, or mother-of-pearl, in sandal wood
and porcelain—mementos of old voyages;
while on the chimney-piece ticked a great
Dutch-looking clock, made in Japan when
none but Hollanders could pass the jealous
cordon of the Nipon custom-house, and
which had accompanied Captain Killick on
many a long cruise. It was hideous to
look upon, this clock, with its yellow face
and the squat metallic ornaments attached
to it, nor was it to be trusted as a time-
keeper; but, singularly enough, its whimsical
master prized it on account of this blemish,
always declaring that it could "give the
go-by" to every clock in the parish, and
averring that although his meddlesome jade
of a housekeeper, Mrs. Curtis, often put
it back an hour or so, its natural vigour

of constitution soon enabled it to make up,
literally, for lost time.

The proprietor and founder of all these
quasi-nautical institutions was by no means,
in personal appearance, what a "fighting
old commodore," like the gouty and shot-
battered hero of a popular ditty, should
have been. The fancy portrait of such a
veteran of the seas was that of some purple-
visaged caricature of Neptune, in cocked
hat and bullion epaulettes, to whom port
wine must surely have been as milk, and
grog as pap, in his infancy; a dilapidated
sea-monster, swaddled in flannel as to his
nether extremities, swearing grisly oaths
against nurse, doctor, and family, flinging
footstools at his wife, and assaulting the
servants with the crutch that lay too ready
to his gnarled and knotted right hand, yet
a generous monster in his milder moods,
and certain one day to provide liberally for
the married daughter who had got into his
black books by wedding a land-lubber. Now
Captain Killick was not purple-faced, cor-

pulent, or mulcted of his full complement
of limbs, neither was he one of the violent
victims of podagra. He was merely a
quaint, sturdy little elderly man, whose
tanned, hale face might as easily have
been embrowned in English harvest-fields
and September stubbles, as by the fierce
sun of the Equator. He had very little of
the sailor in his dress, air, or mien, and
but for his naval tastes and a certain seafaring tone in talking, might have passed
muster as a home-staying gentleman with
a turn for out-door life.

There were two other persons present:
one a fair-haired girl, not very tall, and
perhaps some twenty years of age. This
was Grace, the commodore's niece. The
other was Darrell Conyers, and he rose,
with a laugh, from the tiny table, curiously
inlaid with green jade and many-tinted
shell, the work of Chinese cabinet-makers,
at which he had been playing chess with
Captain Killick as an adversary.

"I could not guess," he said, lightly,

"whom I was to see, or what grand company Sip was ushering in with such dignity."

"Do you call our dark-complexioned friend 'Sip' to his face, Darrell?" asked Craven in some surprise, as he shook hands with Miss Killick.

The commodore took it on himself to answer:—"Indeed he does, Craven, and what's more, the black fellow takes it with wonderful good-humour, like a great cat rubbed down with the grain of the fur. You remember, my dear lad, of course, how touchy and irritable the Coromantee always was at any liberties being taken with his name, or at any one but myself venturing to curtail the word Scipio into the familiar monosyllable 'Sip.' But this boy can go on 'Sipping' all day, without eliciting anything but an extra display of the negro's ivories. The impudent jackanapes has bewitched us all, I think, and had the presumption just now to checkmate me, who might be his grandfather, and taught

him the moves. Deserved to be mast-
headed for checkmating a superior officer,
as I should have been, when I sailed under
old Birtletop! Well, Craven, so you have
come to give your former skipper a look
up, have you, in this snug anchorage of his,
which Sip says, seriously, would be a very
tidy place of residence if it had not the
misfortune to be ashore. How do you get
on with the Admiralty since they paid you
off, eh? Any chance of a crack iron-clad,
or any of the official loaves and fishes
coming your way?"

"Scarcely," Craven opined; adding'that
he ought rather to congratulate himself
on his good luck in having already commanded a gun-boat at so early an age,
than to swell the chorus of complaint
against the heads of the departments, for
not being rapid enough in their recognition
of his superior merits.

"But you'll never be able to reconcile
yourself to stay ashore, boy!" said the
commodore vehemently. "You're not

one of the Queen's hard bargains, of whom,
between you and me, Her Majesty's service
is often well rid, and who loaf and idle
away life on their miserable ten shillings
a day, with an empty jingling title of
captain tacked to their names, to tickle
the ears of landsmen. 'Fore George, sir,
I know some such that I'd hardly care to
put in charge of a watch anywhere beyond
the trade winds, and yet they croak and
bicker at My Lords as if they ought to
be appointed to the Channel squadron.
Never mind that! I'm heartily glad, for
one, to see you back with us for a time,
and you must fix your own day to take a
bachelor dinner here at the Cottage. I
say a bachelor dinner, because Grace there
never presumes to interfere with any of
my arrangements — young ladies never
should. Their business, bless them, is to
look nice and pretty, and go to church, and
play croquet — and I'll try to make you
believe that you are on board the *Thunderbolt* again. I'd bet a hundred pounds you

slaves shackles, given 'em cutlasses, and promised them their liberty if they could repel our boarders; and indeed we had to fight smartly before we could make good our footing, and drive the Dons and their black dupes down below. Well, well, Sip has smelled more gunpowder since than was burned that day, and a braver or more faithful fellow no officer could have asked for at his back."

The commodore himself limped slightly as he walked, a circumstance to which he never alluded, as it would have necessitated the mention of the ounce or two of grape-shot, fired from a Chinese fort, which still remained in his left knee, as a reminder of his former intercourse with the Celestials. But the one subject on which he never bragged was the personal courage which he was well enough known in the navy to have shown on such occasions of con-fronting danger as "little wars," and the suppression of piracy and slave-trading had afforded him. His niece, an especial friend

of Nellie's, talked to her a little in an
undertone, chiefly on local topics; for Grace
Killick was one of those young ladies who,
in an undemonstrative manner, contrive to
do an immense deal of good in a quiet way,
and the children loved her in the schools,
and the aged were glad to see her pleasant
face at their cottage doors.

And then the sloping sun began to indicate that it was time for the commodore's
visitors to go home; and after bidding adieu
to their talkative host, Craven, Darrell, and
Nellie found themselves in the park again,
and walking towards the Towers, the flag-
turret of which, with the silken folds hanging listlessly against the staff, stood out
superbly against the gold and crimson of
the westering sky.

"I always feel after chatting with Grace
as if I were a sad idler, a mere caterpillar,
as it were, living on the leaves, and never
of the least use to other people. She —
Grace Killick, I mean—knows the name of
every child in the school, and has the con-

fidence of the old folks, while I am always forming good resolutions to be very useful, and finding something intervene to bring them to nothing. I really felt ashamed of my supineness just now."

"But you have the notorious excuse of the gentleman who was not affected by the sermon; you 'belong to another parish,'" said Craven smiling; "though I believe the vicarage of Gridley Green, which, by the way, is vacant now, is in my uncle's gift."

CHAPTER IX.

THE RIDE TO THE BEACON.

THE post-bag, which at Crag Towers, and mansions of the order to which Crag Towers belonged, was always forwarded by means of a mounted groom (instead of being left, like the post-bags of minor country gentlemen, with whom horses and men are less plentiful, to the leisurely movements of some pedestrian Mercury, or perchance Iris, from the nearest office), came in, on the day succeeding that of the visit to Captain Killick's cottage, later than was usual. Breakfast, however, was not yet over, and the budget was placed before Sir Peregrine while the family were still at table. The baronet was one of those old-fashioned rural magnates to whom the arrival and distribution of the

household correspondence is not the least
interesting and important event of the day.
It permitted of that kind of dignified trifling
which is very dear to a man who is at once
rich, pompous, and *otiose*. There is many
a family patriarch whom it makes happy to
be, for the nonce, a glorified postmaster,
sorting out, and commenting upon, the
various epistles which arrive, and who pities
in his heart the benighted town-dwellers
whose letters pass the scrutiny of the servants before they reach their destination.
It was always with satisfaction that Sir
Peregrine produced his patent key, unlocked
the bag, and examined its contents. Such
and such letters were for the servants. The
baronet never failed to pore, through his
gold-rimmed glass, over the cramped handwriting of their addresses, and to peruse the
postmarks, before setting them aside to be
fetched away by the butler. He was of a
nature far too honourable to have desired to
pry into the private correspondence of those
who took his wages, although Louis XV.,

whose great amusement it was to help his favourites to rifle the written secrets from the French Post Office, had set him that royal example. But he did like to exercise a mild censorship over the outside of such documents.

The servants' letters being ranged in one little heap, and Sir Peregrine's in another, and the newspapers in a third, the turn of the family and visitor came next. "This is for you, nephew," said the baronet, "and this also," handing to his guest two letters, one of which bore the stamp of Paris. Three for Adeline, two for Nellie, seemed to complete the breakfast-table delivery. But no ; there was yet another envelope, and this the baronet picked up, as he brought to bear on it the focus of the gold-rimmed glass. It was addressed to his grandson, in a large, formal hand, abounding in those lengthy and uncertain upstrokes and downstrokes which ingenious diviners of character by penmanship assure us to be the signs of a weak and vacillating

spirit. Now there is no greater test of the
esteem in which the young of both sexes
are held by their seniors than the respect
paid to the privacy of their cȯrrespondence.
Fred's or Ernest's letters are, it is true, no
longer looked upon as public property, to
be read aloud for general edification, as
was the case with those of the Tommies
and Harries of a bygone generation. Nor
do the elder sisters any longer insist on
looking over the shoulder of sixteen-year-
old Lucy as she unfolds the crossed and
closely-scribbled epistle of some dear darling
schoolfellow ; but, "What is your friend's
good news, Lucy ? " or, "Who's your correspondent, Freddy, my boy ? " still in some
families asserts, half jocosely, the right of
parents and guardians to supervise the correspondence of those who are not yet tacitly
emancipated from control. It was not so
very long since Nellie, in answer to some
such query, had been wont blushingly to
submit her letters to a momentary inspection on the part of Sir Peregrine, who was

a stickler for old-world ways and the right
divine of fathers to bear rule. And this
was the sole envelope that had yet reached
Crag Towers with young Darrell's name
upon it.

"For you, Master Darrell!" was all that
the baronet said, as he tossed the letter
towards his grandson. He had not ogled
the postmark, or criticized the handwriting,
as he had done with the missives for the
servants' hall and still-room; and he at once
addressed himself to his own papers and correspondence, asking Darrell no question as
to the name of the person who had written
to him, or as to its contents. Adeline's lip
curled scornfully as she noted this relaxa-
tion of domestic discipline, but the boy
seemed quite unconscious of the practical
compliment which his grandfather's confidence conveyed, and he read his letter,
folded it, and put it in his pocket, with
an untroubled air and an impassive coolness that belied his years.

It had, on the previous evening, been

planned that Sir Peregrine's two daughters
were to make a rather long excursion on
horseback under the escort of Captain Conyers and of Darrell, which latter had been
authoritatively pronounced by the experienced stud-groom to be deserving of his
master's degree in the difficult art of equi-
tation. The party had arranged to ride
out to a distant point of rising ground
whence a remarkable prospect was, in clear
weather, to be seen, and the horses were
duly ordered for the hour of three. That
morning Darrell had devoted to fishing in
the lake, and he was returning thence
across the park, followed by the under-
keeper and a lad, bearing nets and creels
fairly filled with striped perch and red-
finned roach, amidst which, here and there,
gleamed the green and silver of a pike
ensnared by the trimmer, when he was
encountered by his Cousin Craven, who
said something to him as to the view, on
that day, which they might expect from
the Welsh Beacon. The boy, a very un-

usual circumstance with him, gave a little start of unfeigned surprise.

"I had forgotten the whole thing," he said, and then more constrainedly added : "I have been tiring myself, rather, sculling the boat and racing after those trimmers, without a thought of the long ride of the afternoon. I hardly think I shall care to go so far to-day."

The captain heard this prudent remark with some astonishment, such as we all feel when any one speaks in a manner inconsistent with our estimate of his character. "*You* tired, Darrell; *you* not up to a long ride on a pleasant day like this!" said Craven half incredulously; "I never in my life saw a youngster of your years whom I would so soon back for a heavy bet to run till he dropped—not that I would ask you to tax your strength unfairly," he added, in the considerate way in which he sometimes spoke to those much older or younger than himself.

The boy coloured to his broad white

brow. " I'll go, cousin," he said, "and if I knock up on the road, you can but canter on and leave me to shift for myself. After all, I shall have an hour to rest, and after luncheon I dare say I shall be quite fresh again." So saying he walked on.

" I say, Peters," said the captain half reprovingly to the under-keeper, "why do you let Master Darrell rack himself to pieces in tugging at that heavy tub of a boat, single handed? He's only thirteen, you should remember."

" He *will* do it, captain, and not I, nor any of us, can gainsay him when he chooses to do a thing, and that's the truth," said the man, with evident sincerity. "But the queer part of it is, sir, that, though he took the lion's share of the work, in spite of all I could put in to moderate it, it is quite news to me, I do assure you, about his feeling beat, or that, after it. His muscles, for a young one, are just like steel, and there are not many, under twenty, would care to give and take a hand grip with him. That big bull-headed Tom Morgan, Farmer Morgan's second son, is turned seventeen, and large-boned, too, and made a joke of challenging Master Darrell to try that with him. It was a caution, though, to see Tom grin as though he enjoyed the sport, all the time wringing his great paw as if it had been nipped in a smith's vice; and, if you will believe me, captain, I saw the blood ooze from under young Morgan's finger-nails, while our young master was as cool as a cucumber."

"Ah, well; he's game to the backbone, and will make a fine man, with proper care," answered Craven, turning away; and he thought no more on the subject until the period after luncheon, when, according to agreement, the younger members of the Conyers family were mounted and riding up the road.

"All right, eh, Darrell?" said his good-natured cousin in a low voice, as he reined up his horse beside the boy. And with a cheery laugh Darrell replied in the affirmative.

The day, as Craven had remarked, was a bright and pleasant one, with no threat of rain in the few fleecy islets of cloud that dappled the azure of the sky. The dancing sunlight played gaily on leaf and sprouting corn bladé, and made the rippling waters of the pellucid river glisten like moving diamonds. The very jingle of the bridles had somewhat of a festive sound in it, as the equestrians sped merrily along. Adeline Conyers, who was not of a nature to do anything, as the saying is, by halves, rode very well indeed. She was one of those bold and graceful horsewomen who sometimes lose half the credit of their courage because of the apparently careless ease of their performance.

Nellie, as might have been expected, was by no means equal in the saddle to her taller and more daring sister, but this was not a circumstance which was calculated to occasion any great dissatisfaction to Craven Conyers as he rode beside his pretty cousin's bridle-rein, eager to watch over

her safety in case of need, and glad of the
fair excuse for showing her from time to
time those attentions which every lady on
horseback has the right to expect from the
most heart-whole cavalier whose privilege it
may be to be her temporary estort.

All the party from Crag Towers were well
mounted, for Sir Peregrine's stables were
excellently well maintained. The baronet
had himself, though he rode a dozen or
fifteen miles every day of his life, never
been a sporting, or even what in some
circles is called a "horsey" man. Four
or five times in the course of each hunting
season he made it a point to encourage
the noble science by appearing at the covert
side, and generally rode through the earlier
part of the run by the side of Squire Buckthorne, master of the mottled pack. But
at the first check, Sir Peregrine invariably
tightened his rein and raised his hat with
old-fashioned politeness, taking an urbane
leave of hounds, huntsmen, and fox. He
kept up a well-supplied ·stable, however,

as has been said, partly on the same principle that made him support all races, county assemblies, and the like, as something incumbent on the first commoner in the shire, and partly because the Conyers stock had been, as a rule, mighty hunters and passionately fond of the chase. The wiry little horse which Darrell rode, a black thoroughbred, fit only for a light-weight rider, but full of fire and mettle, and which had been a present from his grandfather, was by no means the worst, although the smallest, of the steeds that made up the sum total of the cavalcade. The boy himself rode on as merrily as the rest, and certainly without betraying any outward sign of fatigue, while it would have been impossible for any one less prejudiced than was the elder Miss Conyers to have refrained from feeling some genuine admiration for the surprising rapidity with which the new-comer among his highly placed kindred had learned to sit and handle his horse.

"Black Sprite seems in a mischievous
temper to-day, Darrell," said Craven, in a
low voice, as they skirted the river; "I
should advise you not to let him fret and
fidget more than you can help before we
get upon the turf." And indeed there was
a wicked gleam in the horse's expressive
eye, while the white froth that studded his
bit, and the manner in which he bounded
from side to side of the road, chafing against
the rein, warranted the captain's well-meant
caution.

"All right!" answered Darrell, with a
quiet smile; and Craven, who saw how
secure was the boy's seat, and how light
and firm was his grasp upon the rein,
pushed on to his former place by Nellie's
side and thought no more of the matter
until, long after they had crossed Battle
Bridge and ridden for a considerable distance among the deep lanes which led towards the hilly country on the opposite side
of the river, he turned and saw with some
surprise that Darrell was not of the party.

"Seen him? not I, indeed," answered Adeline, with that provoking air of indifference that she always assumed when mentioning the detested intruder; "I suppose he has strayed off somewhere, to seek more congenial society at some farmhouse."

"I hope it is no worse, sister, than what you say," rejoined Nellie, with a look of alarm; "you forget how young the boy is—only a child, after all, and unused to riding until so very lately, and that horse of his, too! I should like to turn back and make sure that all is well."

"Oh, there is no doubt of that!" exclaimed Craven, affecting a confidence which he certainly did not feel. "He must be hanging back, somewhere, but the groom is with him, and——" But at this instant the groom in question came up at a hard trot, conscious of having lagged behind, and observing the captain's beckoning gesture, changed his pace into a hand gallop.

"Beg pardon, sir," said the servant, touching his hat as he drew rein; "I had

to go round for a moment to give an order
at the blacksmith's—yonder by the 'Three
Shoes' public." The man omitted to mention that he had wiled away a good many
moments over the convivial pewter, before
the door of the above-named hostelry, where
he had encountered certain brother grooms
exercising their masters' hunters; and that,
feeling awfully guilty as he noticed the
flight of time, he had ridden sharply to over-
take the company ahead of him, in hopes
that his lingering over the stirrup-cup
might pass unreproved.

"Do you know what has become of
Master Darrell?" demanded Craven impa-
tiently.

No. The groom did not know. He had
not seen the young gentleman since they
passed the guide-post at the cross roads;
indeed he was not quite sure whether he
had seen him, to take notice, since they
passed Brooks' End, and that was a good
three mile nearer to the river. Further
interrogated, the man admitted that the

animal which Darrell bestrode, and which was notoriously of a fiery temper, had been plunging considerably when last he saw the boy, "for certain," insomuch that he, Robert, had offered a word of respectful counsel. "Get on, Robert; Sprite and I understand one another, never fear!" had been the cheery response of "Master Darrell." And that was all the man of belt and boots had to relate. "You see, miss," he added, self-excusingly, "Master Darrell not being, like most young gentleman of his age, a bit awkward and timid on a hot horse, and seeing that my nag began to caper, too, for company, why I——"

"You left him to take care of himself. If he has not done so, the fault is his," put in Adeline, in her most trenchant tone, adding, "The child's conceit makes him fancy he can do anything."

"Well, he *have* the heart of a lion!" blurted out clumsy Robert, and then reddened and touched his hat, as he noted Adeline's frown.

The captain was fairly puzzled. No man's heart was softer, where pity for the weak was concerned, than his. And yet he had by far too much of manly common-sense and experience not to be aware that the surest way to spoil a boy is to keep him in perpetual leading strings, and to manifest constant anxiety lest he should come to harm. Out of how many scrapes had he himself, like most midshipmen and public school boys, contrived by good fortune or shrewd mother-wit to flounder, and was he to treat Darrell, the brightest youngster he had ever seen, as timorous mothers treat the urchins whose pranks and love for adventure they can never be brought to understand to be the indispensable adjuncts of healthy boyhood! Perhaps Miss Con-yers was right. Perhaps the lad had found the ride a dull one, and had diverged to some farm or other where his own popu-larity and his prospects as heir would ensure him a delightful welcome. But then, that rearing, buck-jumping brute might have

rolled over with him, or fallen back upon
him, or dragged him by the stirrup, and
while the rest of the company remained
inert the poor boy might be stretched, pale
and bleeding, at the roadside. Craven
scarcely knew what to recommend.

Nellie's vote was that the party should
retrace their steps. Adeline derided the
idea, until she saw, and bit her lip to see,
that Craven was very much disposed to be
guided by her sister's advice, and that he
too was obviously uneasy on the truant's
account. Instantly she joined her voice
to that of Nellie in advocating a prompt
return. They began, therefore, to ride
towards the castle, but at no quick pace,
since Craven thought it advisable, now and
again, to despatch the well-mounted groom
up this or that cross lane to gather tidings
from hamlet or isolated cottage as to Darrell's having passed that way. Ever and
anon, too, he himself pushed his horse
through some gap in the hedge, and rode
to a headland or knoll which commanded

a view of the fields around, waving his
handkerchief, and calling aloud, although
without eliciting an answer or catching a
glimpse of the missing one. Robert's
inquiries proved fruitless. Nobody had
seen the boy whom, by this time, almost
every one know. The fish-hawker passing
in his light pony cart, the wagoner returning with his team, the weeders at work
among the wheat fields, the children gathering posies in the green lane, had seen
nothing of " Master Darrell."

In the meanwhile Adeline's versatile
humour had changed, and she was now in
a perverse mocking mood, which sorely
tested Craven's patience, the rather that it
manifested itself in speculations, to say the
least of them, ill-timed, concerning the
missing boy. " Depend on it," she would
gibingly say, " all that remains of our exemplary nephew is the remembrance of his
high deserts; that, and the task, the melan-
choly task, of dragging the river till we find
the pool where the heir and hope of Conyers

is food for fishes. It must have come, one day or other, so we may as well bow our heads in resignation, and make the best of it."

"What must come? and what do you mean, cousin?" asked Craven bluntly. "I feel anxious, and that, about the lad, and should have hoped you too did so, lightly as you talk of what may turn out to be no laughing matter."

"What should I mean," returned Adeline, with her hard, ringing laugh, "except the curse of Conyers—the Doom, the Fate, or whatever you please—by which this precocious brat is to expiate the sins of our unscrupulous ancestry. You must have heard of the legend, surely, when you were a boy here yourself?"

"I rather think I do remember it," said Craven, after a moment's thought. "At least I recollect its general purport. Excuse me if I say that it seems no fit subject for a jest, at any rate." He had spoken severely, almost sternly, and for the moment Adeline's eyes quailed under the reproach that his conveyed, but not precisely for the reason to which he accredited her temporary confusion. "I like him best so." Such was her unspoken thought. "I never saw him look so handsome as now that he is angry and disgusted at my heartlessness. Ah! if he would indeed be my master and my guide, perhaps I——" Her silent self-communing was interrupted by the return of Robert, the groom, beside whose foaming horse there walked slowly, and with difficulty, the tall figure of an aged peasant woman, in one of those red cloaks peculiar to rustic England, and old England—a picturesque mantle growing yearly rarer and more rare, and soon to be as extinct as the cave-bear or the Dinornis.

"This good lady, sir, though not knowing our Master Darrell by head-mark, seems to have met him," said Robert, by way of explanation, as the tall old woman made her stiff salutation to the young ladies, and stood with her steady china-blue eyes

fixed on their faces, waiting to be questioned.
She was herself, as a type of a fast
vanishing race, a study worthy of a painter.
Old women, doubtless, of all degrees, we
shall always have amongst us, but not for
very long the last surviving specimens of
that self-respecting, quaintly polite, cottage
dame, who did the honours of her humble
dwelling with a stately simplicity that a
princess might have envied, wholly devoid
of vulgarity, because of her steady straightforward train of thought and freedom from
pretension. This particular old woman in
her red cloak, with a covered basket on her
arm, and wearing a preposterous bonnet of
coarse straw, was to all appearance quite
as composed as Adeline Conyers herself.
"Yes," she said, in answer to Craven's
inquiry. "Yes, I took notice half an hour
or more ago, of a young gentleman on a
black horse, as you describe him, I had
never set eyes on him before, but I had
heard talk in the country side of Sir
Peregrine's grandson coming home to the

Towers, and, directly I saw him, I said to myself, you're a Conyers, young sir, by your face. A fine face too; a beautiful one I'd have said had it belonged to a young lady, and yet it had a strange careworn look too, as the boy went by, his reins loose, and gazing straight before him as though it were a ghost he was looking at so fixedly. I am sure he did not see me, although he passed close to me."

"He must be ill—ill and faint, poor child," exclaimed the tender-hearted Nellie.

"Pray tell me, as quickly as you can, where you saw him, my good friend, and in which direction he was going?"

"I had come over Battle Bridge, and walked, I dare say, a goodish half-mile, to Sutton's Bar," answered the old woman, "when he overtook me, close to where the old turnpike stood; and hearing the hoofs of his horse I turned my head. He was riding in the direction of what people call, Wild Will's Ford."

"Wild Will's Ford!" repeated Craven;

"why that, unless I mistake, is that peculiarly dangerous part of the river, below the rocks and the salmon pools, where our ancestor of dubious repute, Wild Conyers, was drowned in the days of Henry VIII., swimming his horse across the Wye in chase of a hunted stag. What can have taken the boy there?—but this is no time for shilly-shally or to speculate. We had better go on, and at best pace too!" And the whole party started at a gallop, taking the road to the river.

CHAPTER X.

UNDER THE PULPIT ROCK.

SOME two miles distant from Crag Towers, but on the opposite side of the river, was a congeries of heaped-up rocks, of bold and fantastic outlines for the most part, border- ing upon and in most places overhanging the swift stream that flowed at their feet. This jumble of tiny grottoes, fairy cliffs, and miniature ravines, was in the tourist season a favourite site for picnics, and doubtless obtained the honour of mention in the local guide-book. As yet, however, the time had not arrived when artists, barristers, and miscellaneous members of the hundred subdivisions of the working world should rush down from heated Lon- don to sketch, row, lounge, or angle in the peerless Wye valley. Accordingly a more secluded spot could not well be found than the vicinity of Wild Will's Ford, from the deep black salmon pools above, to the rapid rush of the narrowing waters below. In the midst of the jumbled, tumbled mass of stones which might (so confused and crowded were the water-worn boulders that composed them) have been flung there by the hand of a sportive Titan, was one notable crag, beetling very slightly towards its bald crown, but as smooth and perpendicular below as if it had been squared by the mason's chisel. This was known traditionally by the appellation of the Pulpit Rock.

Under the shadow of this tall slab of stone, pacing backwards and forwards, with slow irregular steps, along the narrow strip of shingly beach that skirted the fast-flowing Wye, was a man, whose stooping shoulders and drooping head told that he was lost in thought, just as his dejected aspect betrayed that the subject of his meditations was of anything but an agreeable nature. He was dressed in black, and showed some signs of the clerical profession, but his clothes were ill-made, and his cravat badly arranged, so that it was necessary to look at him twice before deciding on his precise social grade. That, if in orders, he was engaged in some secular employment, was tolerably clear. For there are two kinds of clerics—the smartly set-up, neat soldier of the church militant, whose sable uniform and spotless cambric reveal his calling at a glance; and the clergyman who has grown almost to forget that he has the right to wear gown and bands, and who attaches the vaguest meaning to the formal prefix of Reverend on his visiting card. But the rusty black garments and the crumpled cravat, and the thick-soled boots were those of Mr. Meanwell, the tutor; and Mr. Meanwell's pale and perturbed face it was that was turned towards the quarter whence the tinkling of horse's hoofs on the gravel caught his ear. In the next instant Darrell rode up,

yourself to be seen here, and recognized by some servant who remembers your stay at the Castle?"

This speech, considering the former relations of him who uttered it, and him to whom it was addressed, was sufficiently irreverent and deserving of rebuke. It was even more so, when it is borne in mind that Mr. Meanwell was not merely the old teacher, but actually the uncle of the boy before him. But the tutor's tone was one of expostulation, not of reproof, as he made answer: "Indeed, indeed, I thought of such a risk, and took my precautions accordingly. I did not take my ticket for the station whence it is usual for railway travellers to reach Crag Towers. I alighted at a smaller stopping-place, and have come thence on foot, for a distance of some miles;" and he glanced at his dust-coloured boots as he spoke; "and without meeting any one but a few farm labourers or the like. I fixed on this remarkable rock as a fit meeting-place, since you may remember

that Sir Peregrine pointed it out to me,
when he showed us the prospect from the
upper part of the park, and described it by
name as——" .

"I guessed as much before you spoke,"
returned Darrell unceremoniously. "You
might, I admit, have chosen a worse trysting-place, but then why select one at all?
Your writing to notify your intention was of
itself an act of imprudence. How did you
know that my old grandfather, the respected
Sir Peregrine, might not have a senile
fancy for exercising his authority as to the
inspection of my letters? If I had not
played my cards well——"

"Well, do you call it?" broke in the
tutor bitterly; and then added hastily, "I
beg your pardon, I am sure, I meant——"

"You meant"—said Darrell deliberately,
"You meant that natural affection would
alone suffice to account for the old man's
indulgence towards his grandson, and that
I had no right to boast of my own management in the matter. Be it so, I am but

a boy, as you are aware—a mere child,
strange to the world and its guile, and
it is no wonder if my head has become
slightly affected by prosperity and adulation,
is it?" To this the tutor made no direct
reply, but his stolid, puzzled stare of hopeless
astonishment must have had an eloquence
of its own, for Darrell's laugh was one
of genuine mirth as he said : "We didn't
come here, either of us, to bandy words, did
we? In plain English, my dear Mr. Meanwell, why have you sought this interview?"

Thus questioned, the tutor seemed to find
it difficult to frame his reply. He pulled
down his hat over his brows, and with his
hands clasped together behind his back,
walked hurriedly to and fro, his mouth
twitching painfully, and his eyes bent on
the ground, while the boy watched him
with an amused interest, which presently
changed to irritation.

"Now good uncle of mine," he said,
in his clear ringing voice — "for we
ought to forget, none of the Conyers'

stock being here to play chorus to our little drama; that you are, after all, my near kinsman, as well as my old tutor—if you will give up taking 'seven hasty strides,' like the usher in Hood's poem of *Eugene Aram*, and attend to business, we shall have the more chance of coming to a satisfactory conclusion. Pray let me know the nature of your errand—has anything happened?" these last words were very sharply spoken, and Mr. Meanwell, as if unable to withstand their force, turned his haggard face towards the dauntless one of the bright boy, and said groaning—

"No, no—nothing, that is, of consequence. Nothing that *you* would consider as such. But it is a terrible thing to bear about, night and day, a burden of care that grows heavier with every sunset and every day-break. It is a terrible thing to feel sleep banished from the weary eyelids, to toss, restless and fevered, through the miserable night, and to awake feeling as if each man or woman that I meet must read in my

careworn looks and downcast brow, the
secret I fear to betray. I am like Orestes."
But here, to the poor tutor's dismay, his
heartfelt utterance was interrupted by
Darrell's cruel laugh of intense amusement.

"You, dear uncle, to compare yourself
to Orestes!" cried the boy, as a motion of
the rein caused the black thoroughbred
to rear, arrow-straight, in a manner that
would have unseated many a dashing Hyde
Park cavalier, but which appeared to pass
unnoticed, by Sir Peregrine's heir, who
went on, unruffled, with his half-mirthful,
half-bitter speech. "You, of all men, to
compare yourself to that young classical
party over whom you and I spent, I won't
say wasted, many a shining hour. Cannot
the Eumenides, if such there be, stick to
the chase of different game, of a quarry of
another sort—say myself, for instance!"
And as he spoke the last words, at the same
time mastering the revolt of his fiery little
horse by the combined use of hand and

knee, he looked as gracefully beautiful as
Alcibiades in his boyhood may have done
when riding his African barb through the
crowded Agora of Athens.

Mr. Meanwell grew paler yet; and there
was something of genuine pathos in the
very way in which he wrung his large
knuckled hands, with his light-coloured,
uncertain eyes fixed on the fair bold face of
the child who seemed to be his master.

"There is more than that," he said
hoarsely. "More, I mean, than has reference
to my own feelings or the wretchedness of
my life. I have had a letter from the
lawyers—you know what I mean—from
Nupen and Smink, of Gray's Inn."

"Ah, indeed!" Darrell bent forward now,
to listen eagerly, and, as if mechanically,
his hand caressed black Sprite's arching
neck, and straightway, as if there had been
magic in the touch, the fretful horse was
soothed into almost quiescence.

"They have sent me—me! the usual
half-yearly payment—the hundred pounds,"

continued Mr. Meanwell, in the same muffled tone as before. "What was I to do?"

"Do? put the cash into your pocket, and send a formal acknowledgment. *La belle affaire !*" returned Darrell scornfully, and Sprite bounded and snorted as though there had been some mysterious link between horse and rider. "I suppose you have not travelled from Yorkshire to tell me that?"

"No, but to make over this accursed money," answered Mr. Meanwell, looking his former pupil full in the face, " to yourself —unless, indeed I am to send it back. As for keeping it, as for mixing it, unearned, with the little I get by hard work and ill-requited scholarship, I would sooner perish of want by the way-side, than be guilty of what you suggest. I am, at any rate, honest."

"Who ever doubted it, old friend?" said the boy, all his face softening under the bright smile that suited his years so well.

"You come of a good, thrifty, honourable stock, and your forefathers were sturdily intent on saving what they had earned, while mine, on the paternal side, lived by tribute, spoil, and ransom. To send the money back is tantamount to bringing an attorney's clerk down to where you live, and therefore is hardly prudent. I mix a good deal now with gamekeepers, but I never hear, in my studies of natural history, of a rabbit that invites the ferret to his burrow."

"Yet what can I do?" exclaimed the Reverend Mark, striking his open hand upon the rock near him. "Without you at my elbow I am helpless. So long as you were yonder, urging me on, I could make light of riveting on a chain of falsehood, of which every link is a lie; but now I am thinking, do you know, of going as a missionary somewhere—say to China, or the South Seas. I might in that new life be of some good in the world, and forget——"

"And forget me and my affairs," interrupted Darrell, whose features were now hard enough. "I should say, amen! were it not that at the first touch of jungle fever, or home sickness, you would blunder out, to the nearest of your reverend brethren, or the bishop, or the doctor, much that is best untold. No, no, my dear teacher, I cannot spare you to our dark-skinned brethren, among the cocoa-nut trees, far away. I have not gone so far, dared so much, to be checked now by so pitiful a stumbling-block as the weak will of a north-country curate."

As if the black horse had been a familiar demon that heard the words and gloried in their purport, it suddenly began to plunge and fling and rear, steed and rider falling into a succession of attitudes, all perfect of their kind, each of which, but had it been transferred to solid bronze, would have earned deathless immortality for the sculptor who should have set it up in the public place of a great city. Mr. Meanwell grew very white as he stared, with an odd mingling of terror, admiration, and dislike on this boy-centaur, who seemed steeled against all the ordinary weaknesses which we condone in the young.

" Come," said Darrell imperatively, after a hasty glance at his watch, " you have not much time to lose, sir, in regaining your station and starting homewards. The train, going northwards, will pass it by six at latest, while I too shall be missed if I do not ride as fast as fire itself can travel back to the Towers. There is one enemy to keep an eye on me ever, and a trifle might give her the chance she longs for."

" An enemy! who can that be?" asked the tutor with a keen interest.

" It is Adeline Conyers—it is my precious aunt," rejoined Darrell savagely, and speaking through his set teeth: " she has stood, to the utmost of her power, between Sir Peregrine's doting fancy and myself, but the day may come—no matter! Even the boors about this place are learning fast that

it is better to be a friend than a foe, young
as he is, to Daredevil Darrell."

"Oh! boy, dear, dear boy!" exclaimed the
tutor almost with a sob, "be ruled for once,
and hearken unto me. Let right be done,
and all be told at any cost, save that of conscience. I know, I well know," he added
rapidly, "on whom the blame will fall, and
deservedly so. All on me—me, and so be
it! Better bear censure, disgrace, punishment, than days without rest and nights
without slumber."

"I sleep soundly enough," said the boy,
with a mocking laugh; "you should get
your doctor to prescribe you opiates, learned
sir, or, better, walk your twenty miles a
day that the fatigue of your muscles may
overcome the twitching of your nerves.
Have you no shame, bearded man that you
are, to be here whining to a stripling like
myself, destitute even of the ruffian's dogged
boast to 'die game,' frightened rather than
repentant, and of what? Go home for the
present, at all events; later on, I may con-

trive to see more of you. My grandsire has dropped hints already as regards my future education, by which I gather the drift of his wishes; but go home, and quickly. Those lawyers must have their customary answer —you heed me? As for the money, give it me, if you will. It may be of use—ready cash is a valuable tool, sometimes, in skilful hands, and I have but a sovereign left me of Sir Peregrine's last gift."

He stooped forward in the saddle, took the thick roll of bank notes which Mr. Meanwell, with shaking fingers, held out to him, and thrust it into his pocket, then again glanced at his watch.

" They will have observed my absence, turned back, and outstripped me, should we dally more," he exclaimed. " Let me see you start, before I spur for the Towers. Good-bye, tutor, uncle, but don't linger; do you hear me? I will write."

The tutor leant against the rock, passing his heavy hand across his heated brow, while his trembling lips grew white and his

limbs shook, like those of some ague-
stricken wretch. With an effort, he
gathered himself up.

"May the Heaven above us forgive you,
and soften your hard young heart!" he said,
and without further leave-taking wended his
way from beneath the rock and so on till he
reached the dusty high road. There he
turned and waved his hand in sign of farewell. Darrell carelessly returned the gesture, but never relaxed his watchfulness
until the retreating figure was lost to sight.
Then he gathered up his reins and wheeled
his horse. "No time for Battle Bridge,"
he said, as he rode out from among the
stones, "so I must choose a shorter cut
here. This is Wild Will's Ford. Here my
scampish, red-handed kinsman came by his
death three hundred years ago, and every
clown about here has shunned the crossing
ever since. How nervous Sir Peregrine
would be, should he see me now, as to the
Doom being fulfilled. In with you, Sprite—
nay, no denial!" And with hand, knee, and

spur, he forced the snorting, struggling horse into the rushing water, which instantly rose to the saddle-girths. A moment more and the black steed was swimming for dear life, breasting the rapid stream.

CHAPTER XI.

AT FEUD.

"No, miss, not a soul has bent by here, for sartain, on horseback, these twenty minutes," was the response of an old fisherman whose rheumatic pains had been more than once assuaged by port wine and red flannel from Crag Towers, and who now meekly uncovered his thin grey hairs as he answered Nellie's question, "and it has taken me that, and more, to drag the coracle up from the bridge-foot single-handed."

"You know the river well, of course, old gentleman," said Craven, reining up his horse as a thought struck him. "Is there any crossing-place near us, where Master

Darrell Conyers could have got over, without going by Battle Bridge, here ? "

The old piscator, his bundle of rods and gaffs under his arm, and the quaint white linen boat, such as his British ancestors had devised it before ever a Roman legionary planted the eagles on the borders of the Silures and Ordovices, rubbed his shaggy grey eyebrows meditatively.

" The river's pretty full now," he said. " It would take a tallish man, I reckon, and a strong one, to wade even what we call the Shallows, and as for the 'Stepping Stones,' they're under water, and could not be found unless by one of the country folks—nor could a horse keep his feet on them, any day. No, no."

"There's no way of crossing, then ? " repeated the captain, a little weary of the fisherman's prolixity.

"Not above bridge, sir, unless he went by Wild Will's Ford; and no one but a madman would risk that, I'm thinking, with so much water in the Wye," returned the ancient mariner of the stream; and with a nod and a brief "thank you, Owen," the party clattered over the strong stone bridge, once the prize of a fierce battle between Glendower's wild Welshmen and the English levies of Prince Hal.

"It is very clear," said Craven, as they rode briskly on, "either that Darrell passed before yonder old fellow began to haul up his white cockle-shell of a canoe from the river bank, or that he is still wandering among the lanes on the opposite side of the river, having lost his way. And that is the most probable solution of the mystery."

Nevertheless, and although the young man spoke thus confidently, neither he nor Nellie felt by any means reassured as to what had become of Sir Peregrine's grandson. What may have been Adeline's thoughts on the subject remained a secret only known to herself.

"There is no good to be done by our loitering here," said Craven after one or two more inquiries of chance wayfarers had proved fruitless, "so I, for one, propose that we go back to the Towers. Some of the men, in case of need, could go down to the river and——"

"And take ropes," he was going to say, "with them," but he had cut short his speech, first, because he was unwilling further to awaken Nellie's fears, and, secondly, because he felt that, should the boy's high spirit have led him to essay some rash feat beyond the power of horse and man, help would arrive too late. The good-natured young sailor began to take bitter blame to himself for not having taken better care of this, the youthful heir to such bright prospects, the prop and solace of his uncle's declining years. How should he meet Sir Peregrine and tell him that, perchance, poor Edmund's son, the future Sir Darrell, would never be seen more, save when he should be brought in a lifeless, dripping load, to be laid on his bed of death. He wished with all his heart that he had never heard of that tradition of the Curse of

Conyers, a silly, old wife's tale, as he called
it, yet with a comfortless, chilly after-taste
in the memory, too. We can none of us
quite shake off the yoke of our nursery
beliefs, and Craven, though by no means
superstitious, would have given much to
have seen Darrell alive again.

And he had that satisfaction presently,
for on reaching the lodge-gate, an under-
gardener passing out, replied to Nellie's
question by declaring that "Master Darrell
was on the green terrace by the moat." How
long he had been there the under-gardener
knew not, but of the fact, being fresh from
the spot, he was well assured. Dismounting,
the equestrians made their way on foot, still
being incredulous, to the place indicated.
The so-called green terrace was in truth an
elevated ridge of ground, some three bow-
shots in length, reckoning by the arrow-
flight as understood among degenerate
modern toxopholites. It was bounded on
one side by a spreading lawn, and on the
other by the wide moat, being in fact the site

of the ancient barbican, which had defended
the Castle on its landward, or weaker side.
The barbican had been pulled down long
ago; the old moat was dry and choked with
a tangled growth of shrub and bramble and
rank grass, save where two or three deep
pools remained in the broken brickwork,
wherein, beneath a verdant mantle of duck-
weed, carp and tench swam slowly around
the cramped limits of their watery world.
But the terrace, carpeted with the softest
turf, and catching every grateful breeze,
was an agreeable place of resort in hot
weather, while at one end of it was a sort
of tent-shaped structure in the Moorish
fashion, known as the pavilion, and which
afforded a convenient shelter from sun or
rain. In the doorway of this light build-
ing, over the roof of which a profusion of
flowering creepers had been trained, the
figure of Darrell was visible, reclining in a
low American rocking-chair, with one knee
crossed over the other, and with a newspaper
in his hand, the contents of which he was

leisurely skimming. A stray sunbeam
glinted on his golden curls, and then broke
itself upon the gilding of the honey-combed
Morisco arch within—the pavilion had been
gaily decorated with gold-leaf and bright
colours, in true Saracenic style, in compliance with the taste of some bygone
Conyers—and nothing could be, in its way,
more perfectly expressive of repose than the
boy's attitude. He started with a look of
bewildered surprise as he became aware of
the near approach of his late companions.

"You back here, and already!" exclaimed
Darrell. "Why, I could have wagered you
were at the Welsh Beacon by this."

"I am so glad," said Nellie, somewhat
incoherently, as the tears again rose unbidden in her gentle eyes, and then her lips
moved silently as she gave thanks for the
truant's safety.

The younger Miss Conyers was fond of
her young kinsman, although he rarely
bestowed much of his conversation on her;
and, besides, Sir Peregrine! She divined in

the quick sympathy of her tender heart, how dear the young heir was growing to the sonless old man.

" And I am glad," said Craven, " to see you safe and sound, old fellow. A pretty fright and a sharp scamper you have given us."

"I have given you a fright—I?" said Darrell, springing up from his languid attitude, and looking first at one face and then at another, as if endeavouring to guess some enigma. " Why, is it possible you have cut short your ride on my account? Didn't that stupid old farmer give the message so as to be intelligible, then? He made sure of overtaking you when I turned back."

" No, dear, there was no message given by anybody," answered Nellie gently, " we feared you had lost your way, and been thrown, or perhaps had been rash enough to attempt to cross the Wye by fording, and so——"

"And so we lost our excursion, and a splendid view and pleasant gallop, through being absurd enough to encumber ourselves with a young gentleman who consults no one's wishes except his own, and who has not even the good manners to express regret for the annoyance and the anxiety that his whimsical behaviour has occasioned."

It was Adeline who spoke thus, with heightened colour and a frown on her fair forehead; angrily cutting at the standard rose-tree near her with her gold-mounted riding whip.

"Indeed, aunt, I am sorry to vex you, doubly sorry if I have been unintentionally the marplot who has spoiled your day's pleasure!" answered Darrell, fixing his dauntless blue eyes on those wrathful grey eyes of Adeline. "And I am sure I beg pardon of you all if I made you alarmed and anxious about me. But I thought it was all right, when that old fellow in the gig—Jowler, Jolter, or some name like that, as I believe; he's a tenant of the Nevilles, and had met me at Newport's farm when they drew the fish-pond—promised to tell you that I felt just a little fagged, and preferred to turn back. I can't conceive how he missed you, but I'm sincerely sorry if you are offended by my coming home so early."

It was impossible for any words to be more frankly spoken, or to conceive a bearing more marked by graceful candour than that of Darrell. Even to the hostile mind of Adeline the very ring of his voice carried conviction. His blue eyes were as limpid and as steady as those of truth herself. His manner of expressing regret for the inconvenience which he had caused could hardly have been cavilled at by a Chesterfield of our own time. Whatever may have been formerly the case, we in Britain are not very deft apologists, and suffer cruelly under the torture of putting into language the sentiments which our predecessors would have clothed in grandiloquent periods. Miss Conyers, in spite of her violent prejudice, admitted to herself that the young heir of the house, cut off in childhood from all the advantages which wealth and culture bestow, had behaved thoroughly well, and that his manner was as faultless as though he had trodden palace floors from infancy, and been trained under the jealous care of court marshals and high chamberlains. And that, at Darrell's age, is so difficult. It is almost necessary to have been a boy, and to have preserved, in all their freshness, the recollection of boyish miseries, boyish mortifications, to realize how hard it is for a boy's demeanour to merit praise; how nice should be the tact that enables the youngster in his early teens to steer between the Scylla of passive deference and the Charybdis of rude self-assertion. Now, the peculiarity of Darrell's address was that those who talked with him were apt to forget that he was but thirteen years old, until the fresh young voice, the merry laugh, or the smoothness of the cheek, reminded them that the heir of Crag Towers was scarcely more than a child.

"Bravo, Darrell!" said Craven, patting his young kinsman on the shoulder; "you

were quite right to turn back if you felt that
a long ride up hill and down dale would be
more fraught with pain than with pleasure.
Say no more about it, but some day before I
go we'll pay our visit to the Beacon, and
duly admire the bird's eye view of the five
counties, and have a race, too, if you like,
among the grass rides cut through the
heather. Sprite, with your light weight on
his back ought to hold his own even with that
big chestnut, Lightning, that was selected
for me. But take a sailor's advice, and
don't overdo that rowing exercise of yours.
The oar, like fire, is a good slave but a
hard master, and those broad-built, heavy-
timbered boats take it out of a fellow
whose bones are not set yet, although,
upon my word," he added laughing, as he
took Darrell's right arm between his fingers,
" the muscles are as hard and as elastic as
those of a young tiger. Take care of yourself, and some day it won't be easy to find
your match for sinew and strength."

" Some day!" Darrell murmured over

these words to himself in so low a tone as to
be inaudible to any ear save his own, as he
slowly sauntered towards the house in
company with the rest of the party; and he
glanced upwards quickly at the blue of the
sky and the greenery of the summer foliage,
and the sunshine that enveloped the earth
as in a glory, and then sighed as his bright
eyes assumed the dark and weary look
which from time to time came over them
like a cloud. It is not uncommon for the
young and gifted, even on the threshold of
life, to feel somewhat of the lassitude and
the wish for rest that the aged king of Israel
sang with all the emphasis of experience;
not uncommon, too, for them to anticipate
for themselves the doom of much immatured
promise. It is but a trite and partial
truth that "those whom the gods love
die young." Not every youthful poet has
his sweetest numbers silenced for ever by
the touch of the destroying angel, as befell
Keats and Shelley, Byron and Chatterton·
Not every hero falls like Hoche or Wolfe'

with his first laurels freshly twined around the head that was never to be silvered by old age. But there is something in all precocity that suggests the homely proverb, " soon ripe, soon rotten." The sharpest sword, so armourers say, is that which rusts the quickest.

Darrell's despondent moods were never of long duration, especially when others were near him; and, indeed, he had never before experienced even a momentary darkening of the spirit while the elder Miss Conyers was present. As it was, he instantly rallied, nor did Adeline, whose powers of observation were acute, beyond even the average of her perceptive sex, mark any change in the boy's aspect. As she walked on towards the house she felt half angry with herself, as she thought of her own petulance towards her brother's son, hated for no offence but that of his birth. To her fancy, she had been worsted in an encounter of her own choosing, and the blood mounted to her proud face at the thought that she had been in the wrong, and violent, and that this child whom she detested had· overcome her by sheer command of temper, and that without effort. Some impulse that she could not resist made her turn, as they entered the house, and say, in a voice that was not quite steady, "Come, Darrell, let us be friends! I was angry, and, I am afraid, unjust a little time ago. You must forget it, will you not?" And she smiled as she drew off her white riding glove and offered her jewelled hand to Darrell, who took it, after an instant's hesitation, in his own.

"I'll promise not to think of it," he said, with a light laugh. But when Adeline, who for the moment was really softened towards him, bent down her head to kiss him, he drew back, and let go her hand. "You have never done that," he said coldly, "not when I came here a stranger—not as I came to be known among you. It is too late, now."

Their eyes met, with a flash like that of the steel points of crossing swords as the first pass is exchanged by duellists who feel the quarrel to be a mortal one. Adeline's face crimsoned to the very hair. " The next time that I ask to touch your cheek with my lips," she said, speaking in a voice so low and sibilant that it sounded like the hiss of a serpent, "it must be on my death-bed, or yours." And without another word she turned from him and went in. Darrell stood looking after her with a watchful smile upon his face.

" I suppose," he said to himself, medi-tatively, "that I have been imprudently outspoken, or at least what would be so considered by an impartial umpire. It isn't often that, as the commodore would say, I hoist my colours and fire a broadside at the enemy; but this time I seemed less to utter my own sentiments than to be the mouthpiece of something stronger than myself—a dangerous symptom that, and it shows that I need curb and bit as much as Sprite does. And, after all, I'm not sure that an open breach is not

better than a smouldering state of covert
hostility. That fair foe's power to harm
and thwart will be lessened, not increased, if
pique makes her show her hand too plainly."

Nobody had observed that little scene
between Miss Conyers and Darrell—the
former's overture at reconciliation, or its
repulse; but the haughty Adeline went to
her room, and dismissed her maid from her
customary attendance, lest the tears of rage
that she could no longer keep back, should
provoke the tattle of the domestic censors
below. To be reproved, baffled, beaten, by
an adversary so little fit to cope with her,
who in London and Paris had won applause
by the spirited repartees which had passed
from lip to lip, with her name appended to
them. She had had, like other reigning
belles of the season, to run the gauntlet of
those witlings of whom simple ladies speak
with bated breath as "very clever" men,
and who sometimes take an ill-natured
pleasure in snubbing and puzzling the new
beauty, innocently enjoying the incense of

the general admiration. And there were one or two drawing-room cynics of this sort who grew hot and shamefaced years afterwards, when in private self-communings they remembered the titter of those who heard Adeline return their sneers with telling home-thrusts that left a scar behind. And how had she failed with this boy, this urchin whom she had tried in vain to browbeat, and who had rejected her caress with a frigid courtesy that was more galling than any outburst of juvenile wrath could have been. Yes, no doubt he was right, and friendship was impossible between them; yet they were thrown much together by circumstances, and it was likely that for years to come they would remain household foes, ever at feud, yet sitting at the same board, sleeping beneath the same roof. Had Darrell allowed himself to receive the kiss, that peace offering would probably have been the mere symbol of a truce certain to be broken when two irreconcileable interests, two jarring natures, should next come into collision.

"I should not have loved him one whit the more," Miss Conyers had the shrewdness to add to her soliloquy, "but now I hate him. Oh! how I hate him —the more intensely, perhaps, because I am helpless, and cannot have the poor gratification of despising him. But beware, nephew, how any mad prank, any youthful escapade, comes to my knowledge ere it reaches Sir Peregrine's ears."

What would Adeline have given for the knowledge of how Darrell had reached Crag Towers? the heaving flanks of Sprite giving token of the desperate speed of his homeward race, while his own clothes and the thoroughbred's stained skin were wet and streaked with foam and froth; how he had flung the bridle of his reeking horse to an astonished helper, had hurried from the stables to change his attire, and had but had time to lounge for some few minutes in the rocking chair, under the shade of the pavilion on the terrace, before the unsuspecting companions of the earlier portion

of the ride came up. As it was, the interview with Mr. Meanwell beneath the Pulpit
Rock, and the subsequent swimming of the
river at Wild Will's Ford, remained as
secrets in the safe custody of the discreet
young heir of the mansion.

CHAPTER XII.

A FAMILY COUNCIL.

"I HAVE sent for you, Adeline, my dear, because I wish for the benefit of your opinion on a subject of some importance, not to me alone, but, ahem! to us all. I may go farther, and say to all whose fortunes are connected in any way by ties of interest, or by bonds of friendship, with our house. Burtell, you may take the dogs with you." This last observation was addressed to the servant who, having opened the study door for the entrance of Miss Conyers was about noiselessly to retire, when his master's voice recalled him,— " their whimpering disturbs me."

And then Adeline knew that her father, in requesting her presence in his library,

must have been very much in earnest as to
the fancied importance of the discussion
to ensue, since he had given this order for
the banishment of his canine favourites.
Sir Peregrine's greyhounds never seemed
to distract his attention very greatly when
he gave audience to a farmer who craved
the repair of a barn, or the renewal of a
lease. He was not illiberal as a landlord,
neither was he, in his territorial capacity,
by any means the King Log that a many-
acred magnate, not grasping enough to play
the part of a King Stork, often is. The
tenants, in confidential moments over their
ale and churchwarden pipes, criticized Sir
Peregrine as all of us are criticized by
somebody; but they never said among themselves that he was a bad judge of stock,
ignorant of draining tiles, or otherwise than
cognizant of white crops and root-crops, of
pasture and fallow, and all that relates to
British agriculture. Had it not been for
his weaknesses as to ground game and
pheasant preserves, and his fixed deter-

mination to have his vassals' votes as well
as their rents, he would have been a
tolerable man of business.

But now the whining, fondling brutes
that jumped on their master, and licked his
hand, and watched his every movement, four-
footed courtiers that they were, had been
turned out of the room, and Sir Peregrine
was left with his two daughters. Nellie had
indeed been with her father for some little
time before Adeline's arrival, but her advice,
if asked, had probably not been of great
weight with the head of the family, to
judge by Sir Peregrine's next words.

"Our dear Nellie," he said, kindly patting her little hand, as he would have done
to a child, "has been willing to contribute
her quota of counsel; but I should like,
Adeline, to hear what you have to say on
the subject which now preoccupies my
thoughts—what is to be done with Darrell?"

"Done with him?" Miss Conyers could
not help repeating the words, in evident
surprise. She had not guessed the topic

on which her father desired to speak; nay, she had entertained a wild idea that his wish to consult with her, might have some reference to the matrimonial aspirations of Captain Craven Conyers.

"As refers to his education, I mean," Sir Peregrine condescended to explain. "It is a subject to which I have devoted much thought lately, and I desire, as I said before, to have the help of your advice. Yours is a clear head, Adeline, and I set store upon what judgments you form."

Now this was a compliment, coming as it did from the reserved master of Crag Towers, but Miss Conyers let it pass unnoticed. A tinge of crimson glowed through the creamy whiteness of her fair face, and she beat with one of her small feet upon the carpet, while her hand closed tightly on the back of the chair beside her.

"I am afraid," she said, in her coldest tone, "that my judgment is little worth the having on such a point as the education of a schoolboy."

The baronet, who had been poising a gilded paper-knife, as if intent on ascertaining its weight, appeared unconscious of his daughter's unwillingness to show any interest in the subject proposed to her for discussion.

"I think, my dear," said Sir Peregrine, still weighing the burnished paper-knife— "I think that you undervalue your own ability to decide, and that you are more competent than you imagine to advise me as to the course I should adopt. I must set you right, however, on one minor point. You spoke, an instant ago, of Darrell as a schoolboy. Now the question is, shall he, or shall he not, be sent to school? There is much to be said, no doubt, on both sides, for and against."

"Indeed!" returned Adeline, arching her slender neck in unconscious imitation of a swan that rears her snowy crest from among the reeds and river-flags to confront the intruders that have approached too near to her nest. "I believed there was but one opinion as to the fittest training for a young Englishman of gentle blood. You were at a public school, sir, as you remember, and at the university, yourself. I am presuming, of course, that you do not intend the child to be educated for the army?"

"Certainly not," replied the baronet, letting go his hold of the paper-knife, but instantly resuming it; "our family has given enough of its members to the military profession, and my views for Darrell are widely different. I do not design, in fact, that he should embrace what is called a career of any sort, but content himself with the discharge of those duties to which, at my demise, he will succeed. Unless, indeed, he should hereafter prefer to take that active part in political and parliamentary life from which it has always been my choice to stand aloof."

Now Adeline was usually wary in conversation with her father. She knew well enough that he respected her far more than he loved her; that, so far as natural affection

went, his heart was softer towards her
unassuming younger sister than towards
herself; but that he was proud of her as a
true Conyers, and vain even of her beauty
and her accomplishments. She fancied, too,
that Sir Peregrine was, if not exactly afraid
of her, still disinclined to any direct asser-
tion of his paternal authority where she was
concerned, and that he conceded to her
her own way in many trifles, sooner than
permit that his will and hers should clash.
But she also knew that there were matters
on which the baronet would brook no compromise ; and that one of these, and perhaps
the greatest, was his jealous regard for the
high repute of the ancient stock, the chief-
ship of which belonged to him. She was
ordinarily careful, therefore, not to trespass
on forbidden ground, and would have preferred not to have been consulted on any
topic relative to the young heir. But she
was nettled now, at the constant proofs
of Darrell's high place in Sir Peregrine's
esteem, and could not restrain herself from

saying:—"Well, sir, I see no reason to deviate from the usual system. Send him to Eton first, and then to Christchurch. The authorities of those places will surely be competent to make him fit to take his seat on the magisterial bench, and even to give his vote in the House of Commons. As to the lighter task of drawing the rents of this estate, we need have no fear on that score. School and college, with their wholesome tasks and more wholesome discipline, at any rate prevent a lad from turning out a misanthrope or a milksop."

Miss Conyers did not add to this vigorous tirade the thoughts that supplemented it in her busy brain, and which were to the effect of—"And, once at school, his hated presence will not every day cross my path. He will be absent from the Towers for three-fourths of every year, and who knows if time and habit may not lessen my father's infatuation about this young upstart, and——"

But Adeline's meditations were interrupted by Sir Peregrine, who now said slowly, but with some severity :—

"I am quite as well aware, daughter, of the obvious merits of our public-school system, as it is possible that you should be. I said as much last week to the marquis, and no later ago than yesterday, to Sir Hugh Neville, when they kindly joined me in discussing Darrell's future prospects. But I had hoped that you, as one of ourselves, would have appreciated the reasons for not deeming it indispensable that my grandson should immediately be transferred to one of those seats of learning of which you, and the friends I have mentioned, speak in terms of such, ahem! I am sure, deserved praise. He has no brothers, and all my hopes centre in him. The great fortune which will one day be his, makes special study on his part quite superfluous. At a later period he might be sent to receive the polish of university training, but at present I should prefer that he should remain under my own eye, and receive all needful instruction without quitting the house which will one day be his. And I scarcely think that such a boy as he is runs any serious risk of becoming, as you phrase it, a milksop."

" Perhaps not," answered Adeline, pressing her lip sharply between her pearly teeth, and speaking with a superb disdain. "He may, however, develop into some other objectionable type. Of course you are the best judge. Had not my thoughts on the matter been asked for, I should never have volunteered them."

" I was of much the same mind myself, sister," said Nellie, looking up from the low seat which she occupied beside her father's great armchair; "and for the same reason, I am sure. I really thought Darrell would be happier so, with companions of his own age, but then I know how clever and quick to learn he is, and how——"

" You are all in a conspiracy to spoil the child with flattery and more liberty than would be good for him, were he even the wonder you think him ! " broke in Adeline, flushing crimson with the anger she could not repress. "The cleverest boys sometimes become the most insufferable, when they find themselves turned into little idols, to be worshipped by those older than themselves."

Sir Peregrine frowned, and almost snapped the metallic blade of the paper-knife, as he heard these words. There was something piteous, as well as absurd, in his embarrassment. After all, we may spare a little compassion for even a domestic despot, who finds that the family senate reprehensibly refuses to ratify his decrees. He was now sorely displeased, and somewhat perplexed withal, for it was something new, this open defection on the part of his elder daughter. Adeline had been in the habit of treating him with a studied deference, less akin, perhaps, to filial obedience than to the homage which some great vassal of the Crown might yield to his suzerain. And this impersonal form of respect, paid, as he felt, less to the father than to the chief of the house, had always served to impress Sir Peregrine with a lively sense of what was due to a lady so well versed in her rights and her duties. He therefore began to cast about for some loophole whereby, without any ostensible sacrifice of dignity, he might avert an unseemly contest. Algerian hunters tell us how the lion, confronted by numerical odds, yet unwounded, faces the line of armed men with dauntless front and horrent mane, as if striving, as a wrathful king might do before rebellious subjects, to overawe the enemies by the terrors of his regal frown, and the majesty of his lofty bearing. And yet, if unassailed, the mighty brute approves himself discreet, as well as valiant, for, inch by inch the formidable paws recede, and with his face ever to the foe, his eyes glowing like live coals, his tufted tail slowly beating on the heaving flanks, the lion backs away into the friendly shadow of the thorn-bushes, and gradually disappears, like a dissolving view. Once on the other side of the

thicket, court etiquette and the stage strut
are forgotten, and Leo, his huge head
lowered, and his martial aspect changed,
scuttles away with the life-saving speed of
a strange cat chased out of a dairy.

But Sir Peregrine was much relieved
when aid came to him from an unexpected
quarter. It was not often that Nellie ventured to enter the lists of argument with her
more brilliant sister, but injustice was singularly repellent to her, as it sometimes is
to gentle natures, and she took it upon
herself to reply to Adeline's last words.

"I really do not think," she said, "that
such a way of putting the case is quite
fair to Darrell. He, at least, never presumes on the good-will and favourable
opinion of those around him, and I fear,
Adeline, that you have been too hasty,
and have mistaken his character. Rely
upon it, if he were a beggar-boy in rags,
he would still have that frank nobleness of
disposition which even the veriest stranger

appreciates. Even if we tried to spoil the
boy, I do not believe we could succeed, so
healthy and sincere is his nature. I was
inclined to think that school would suit
him best, but that was because it is sad-
dening for one of his years to be cut off
from the society of those of his own age.
But if he likes better to study at home, I
should say that his feeling on the subject
was worthy of attention."

Sir Peregrine eagerly caught at the idea
suggested by his younger daughter. "I
quite agree with you, my dear," he said
blandly; and as he spoke he touched the
library bell, which was within reach of his
hand. "I shall come to no final decision
until I have learned what my grandson's
desires are on the point in question. Of
course, had he been a lad of another sort,
I should have chosen for him without
scruple. But he is so wise, and so good,
that he does not deserve to be treated as
an irresponsible child. Ask Master Darrell
to come to me for a moment," he added,

to the servant who obeyed the summons of the bell.

"This is too much!" said Adeline, with an accent of genuine indignation that was not lost on the sensitive ear of her father. "It is right that I should retire when such ripe wisdom is summoned to the consultation. After all, so that we are not rendered ridiculous, I care not what may be the result of the debate." And before Sir Peregrine could shape his reply she had swept, in all the haughtiness of offended beauty, from the room.

Darrell was quick in responding to his grandfather's message, and as usual his presence seemed to bring with it, to Sir Peregrine's fancy at least, an element of strength and wholesome freshness. "It certainly seems odd, grandpapa"—he said, with that winning frankness which was peculiar to him—"odd that a lad like myself should have to give his opinion about going to school; and if I were of a lazy turn, such as that of some fellows, I suppose that I should say No, just for fear of the Greek and the algebra, and the discipline and punishments I had heard of. I do say No, but not because I am idle or afraid to rough it. Wherever I am I hope to work and to learn. But I have been so short a time at home—it seems but yesterday, grandfather, since I found you all, and began to be one of you, and part and parcel of the dear old place—that I should like better not to be sent away at once among strangers. That is all."

Machiavelli or Marlborough could not, from the deep quiver of diplomatic experience, have drawn forth an arrow better adapted to hit the mark than this apparently random shot of Darrell's aiming. It was the tone, of all others, in which to address Sir Peregrine, and the baronet's rigid port relaxed a little, and there was a trace of moisture in his usually severe eyes as he listened. He was touched by the affection for himself which the boy's words implied. All his life long had the proud,

silent, exacting man craved for the love of
others, unaware that his jealous reticence
kept such from him as effectually as the
shell of a bivalve excludes the soldier-crab
and the sand-eel. His wife had feared him
too much to be very fond of him. His
brother had regarded him as a banker on
whom to draw for welcome cash. His
younger daughter's affection for him,
stronger than he knew it to be, had
constantly been repressed by his cold dignity of deportment, while he had never
understood the character of Edmund, his
son. One of Darrell's great merits in his
eyes was that he appeared to be growing
attached to his grandfather, and this new-
found treasure of filial love Sir Peregrine
was almost tremblingly afraid to part with.
School-life might nip this affectionate feeling in the bud, and be the first step, not
impossibly, towards bringing about an estrangement between the heir and the owner
of Crag Towers.

"It is possible, of course, that a well-selected tutor, who should devote his abilities entirely to your instruction, might conduct your education with even greater completeness than if you shared the studies of a crowd of boys," said the baronet, as if thinking aloud. "Much, very much, would depend on the appointment of a proper person. The emoluments which I should be able to propose would be worthy the acceptance of even an eminent scholar."

"I should like, with your permission, grandpapa, to be taught by my dear old tutor, Mr. Meanwell," returned the boy quickly; "a better teacher, or a better man, does not live. He and I work together as smoothly as any master and pupil that ever existed."

Sir Peregrine made a wry face at this suggestion. To his fancy, it appeared as if his grandson's tutor should be, at the very least, a Doctor of Divinity, and endowed with somewhat of the polish of that very old school of divines whose manners were of the court, courtly, who quoted

s

Horace over their wine, and talked excessively like men of the world, whose calling demanded a sober decorum of word and deed.

"As for his looks and his awkwardness, poor fellow," continued Darrell, as if he guessed the nature of Sir Peregrine's thoughts, "I do believe you would soon become reconciled to them, sir, in consideration of the sterling excellence beneath. There is something more than honest, downright zealous, rather, in his mode of teaching, which carries the learner along, as I can vouch for, at times when a dull master, or a cross master, or a master who did as little as he decently could, would never keep the boys' attention from flagging. And it isn't only that he spares no pains. There is no doubt whatever that his ungainly habits and bashfulness had held him back from making a figure in the world. I have seen letters from great dons and bishops, highly praising his scholarship and industry, and expressing regret that he had allowed inferior men to distance him in the race. He's poor, you know, and never, at the best, could do much more than pay his way; and I am sure he would thankfully accept your offer, grandpapa, if you would make him one."

Sir Peregrine smiled, and then a cloud came over his brow as he said, "I forgot one feature in the case—the unfortunate connection that exists, through your mother, Darrell, between this Mr. Meanwell and ourselves."

"But he, too, will forget it," answered the boy gaily; "and for that matter, so shall I. He has always seemed as a kind instructor to me, nothing more. And he is not one to presume on the accident of the relationship, while people could not help liking him a bit for his own sake."

Again the baronet's face brightened. "Do you wish this, Darrell?" he asked, with unusual gentleness. " Wish it, I mean, very much indeed?"

"Indeed I do, sir," answered the boy

earnestly; "it would make me even happier than I now am, if possible, if you would kindly agree to such a plan."

Sir Peregrine shook his head, uttering an oracular promise that he would turn the subject over in his mind, and the family council broke up; but nevertheless it was clearly understood that, for the moment at least, the boy had carried his point.

Strange! that he should be so anxious for the society of one whom he had so recently treated with such imperious contumely, beneath the shadow of the Pulpit Rock. But perhaps Darrell's heart had smitten him since then for his harshness towards his old tutor, and he desired to atone to Mr. Meanwell for his rough scorn on that occasion; the young are permissibly fickle in their moods—it might be so.

CHAPTER XIII.

A CASE OF LAY PATRONAGE.

"I DO not mind saying, in confidence, to you, Craven, that I am very much annoyed and distressed by Adeline's conduct in this affair. I promised, or at least led Darrell to expect, that this old tutor should be recalled to take charge of his education. There were reasons, ahem! why this arrangement involved some concession, some sacrifice of private feelings on my part, since, as you doubtless remember, there is a family tie between pupil and teacher which I would willingly ignore, and the fact of which need hardly be obtruded on public notice. However, since this Mr. Meanwell is of a modest and unassuming disposition, I might have consented to waive that objection, and

Darrell's heart is obviously set upon the resumption of his former studies under their original auspices. On the other hand, my daughter almost forgets the respect due to a father in the vehemence with which she protests against the introduction of this 'uncouth element,' to use her own words, into our family circle. She declares that she will no more submit to accept the constant company of Mr. Meanwell than she would sit down at table with a gorilla. It was a strong expression."

"It was, uncle," returned the young man, crushing down by a violent effort his natural impulse to laugh.

The captain was by far too good-natured not to risk, if necessary, the breaking of some small blood-vessel under the spasms of suppressed merriment, rather than mortify the baronet by an untimely burst of cachinnation. And just then the master of Crag Towers was in no mood to appreciate mirth. A proud man, in a conspicuous position, and dimly conscious that he has a

weak will, and must reckon with those
stronger than himself, is not to be envied.
And in his way, poor Sir Peregrine had
been through life an impostor, striving to
cheat others and himself into a belief that
he was a sort of Talus with the iron flail,
ready to make short work of all presumptuous opponents. The late Lady Conyers
had taken him at his word. His frigid
haughtiness had chilled her simple, loving
heart from the first; and when the time came
for her to turn her face to the wall she had
not been very sorry that Death's cold grasp
should snap the golden circlet that had been
as a fetter to her. He was known to have
dealt very severely with his eldest son, who
had, so he held, disgraced the Conyers
blazon by marrying a good girl whose name
was unknown to the heralds. But Captain
Edmund, again, had taken him at his word.
Had he, instead of accepting his sentence of
banishment, come boldly down to beard the
dragon in his den, stormed Crag Towers
with his young wife on his arm, and borne

the ordeal of a stormy scene or two, there
might have been no Indian exile at all, and
no lifelong quarrel. The Moloch of pedigree
that Sir Peregrine worshipped was, like
other evil idols, only terrible to those who
bowed the knee.

The baronet was discontented now. That
flaccid will of his, to which allusion has been
made, was being sorely ground as between
the upper and nether millstones, by the
strong wills of Adeline his daughter and
Darrell his grandson. His wishes were on
the side of the latter. Darrell had his
promise. Darrell, in this case, had his
sympathies. But Miss Conyers had de-
veloped an unexpected obstinacy on the
subject of the bringing of Mr. Meanwell to
Crag Towers, and had more than hinted
that if the clumsy tutor became a resident
under that roof she would quit its shelter.
Sir Peregrine knew enough of Adeline's
nature to credit her with being capable of
executing her threat, and therefore stood
aghast at the prospect of a scene and a

scandal. The boy, on the other hand, would not yield an inch of the ground that he had won. He held his grandfather to his word, and Sir Peregrine never deliberately broke or backed out of a pledge. And it always happened that, after a few minutes talk with Darrell, the old man felt that if he permitted himself to be thwarted on this point, he should never again be able to assert his legitimate authority as he had hitherto done. Darrell was himself impassive to all his kinswoman's sarcasms, and in every verbal encounter appeared to have the best of it through his sheer fearless simplicity and unruffled temper. To treat him as a child was impossible. He reasoned too well for that. And yet, as even injustice itself could not have accused him of apeing the ways of manhood, he afforded no mark for Adeline's satire, a good deal of which was expended on the absent Mr. Meanwell.

Domestic discomfort was beginning to tell on Sir Peregrine's nerves and spirits, and it was as a last resource that he conceived the plan of extracting by indirect means the counsel which he was too proud to ask from his nephew. Under pretence, then, of showing the progress made in a new pheasantry among the pine trees, the master of the Towers made a short excursion in Craven's company, and allowed the conversation to turn on Darrell and the imbroglio of his future education. These harmless *ambages* were too transparent to hoodwink the captain, but he was too sincere in his good-nature not to be willing to smooth away, if he could do so, the difficulties in his uncle's path.

"Of course, sir, you are the best judge," said the young commander modestly; "but is there no way of reconciling matters? A separate suite of apartments, perhaps, would suffice to keep this unlucky Mr. Meanwell from offending by his clumsiness and rustic ways, or, stay! He's a clergyman, is he not?"

"Yes, but what can that have to do with the embarrassment which his coming will create here ? " said Sir Peregrine, arching his eyebrows.

" Give him the living of Gridley Green, sir," rejoined Craven smiling. " It is in your gift; and I gather from what you said the other day that you have not yet decided who is to be the new incumbent. I take it for granted he's all right, and could pass the Admiralty—I mean the bishop's—examination. Post him, then, as I wish ' My Lords ' would do for me—turn him from a curate without a curacy into a vicar with glebe and stipend, pulpit and parsonage. He will be near enough then for Darrell to read with him as many hours a day as may be wished, and yet not necessarily a frequent guest at the Towers. I suppose that with the living, and a couple of hundreds a year for tuition, the poor man would be in clover."

The captain's happy device produced the same effect which, during the famous deadlock in the *Critic* results from the expedient of calling on the involved duellists, in the Queen's name, to drop their swords and daggers. Sir Peregrine was glad to assent to an expedient which should save his own dignity while purchasing a respite from those household dissensions from which most educated Englishmen shrink as from the worst of ills. Darrell expressed his satisfaction with the project; and even Adeline was probably not sorry that a compromise should put an end to the conflict between her father and herself. As a neighbour, Mr. Meanwell might be tolerated, she averred, whereas such an inmate of the Castle would be simply insufferable. That the Reverend Mark should thankfully accede to the proposed arrangement seemed a moral certainty. He had never had more than three—more commonly two—pupils at one time under his charge. His literary labours, as is usual with those of a dull, sound scholar, were poorly paid. It was long since he had held a sorrily remunerated north-country curacy. Now the benefice of Gridley Green, although by no means one of the great prizes of Church preferment, was at any rate one of which many a starveling incumbent of those poor and populous parishes that have been carved out in the most disagreeable portions of crowded cities might have thought of with a sigh, as of a land flowing with ecclesiastical milk and honey.

Gridley Green had a parsonage, reasonably roomy and commodious, in good repair, and standing among the black yew-trees and towering mountain-ashes of a garden large enough for the requirements of a clerical Adam, even though there might be many mouths to crave their share of fruit and vegetables. No such apples for miles around as those that hung on the boughs of the old trees, red and russet and green and golden, a very pageant of Pomona's marshalling. The red bricks of the peach wall that faced the south were famed for mellow stone fruit, and the gooseberry and currant bushes were as a jungle. Then the glebe consisted of sixty acres of good land, croft, pasture, and coppice. The pecuniary emoluments were somewhat above the average. The small, or vicar's, tithes of Gridley Green are rated in the King's books, as we may any of us see by a glance at the *Clergy List*, at four hundred and twenty-seven pounds, nine shillings, and eightpence, a year. Those who are knowing in Church matters say that such estimates on the authority of official print are apt to be under, not over, the mark. It may therefore, probably, have been the case that the actual receipts were a little more than £427 9s. 8d. It was certainly a gift worth the taking.

If any one entertained a doubt as to Mr. Meanwell's acceptance of what, to a man in his position, must have appeared as comparative affluence, that person was Darrell.

"You see, grandpapa," he said, when Sir Peregrine had completed his pompous letter to the tutor, and as a mark of extreme condescension had given the grandiloquent manuscript to his heir for perusal; "you see that the poor old fellow is terribly bashful, and full of odd scruples. It isn't, of course, that he will be slow to appreciate the great kindness which you do him, or the immense advantage offered; but it is of his own diffidence that I'm afraid. He never was much used to parochial work, and yet he is not the man to take the pay without performing the duties, especially in a place like this, where there are two chapels, and half the people go to them. So I think, with your leave, that I had better write to urge his compliance. He likes me, and is used to me, and I sometimes fancy that, poor man, he can deny me nothing."

There was something odd, a ring of suppressed meaning, in the tone in which these last words were uttered. Then, too, the fair young face of the speaker wore a singular expression, one of which the baronet, no very acute physiognomist at any time, would have found it difficult to decipher the purport. But he saw nothing,

being a down-looking man. Such persons
as Sir Peregrine, haughty, sensitive, and
unhappy in the isolation to which their
fancied greatness dooms them, rarely, except by a conscious effort, look any one
fairly in the face. There are gentlemen
of wealth and rank who, as they notify
their hurried orders, scan the topmost
button of the head-gardener's coat, criti-
cize the horse-shoe pin in the stud-groom's
flat cravat, and seldom permit their eyes to
travel higher than the apron strings or the
loud-ticking gold watch of the stately housekeeper. Thus it was that Sir Peregrine,
as Darrell spoke, looked at his own letter,
and at the great gold-mounted seal, cut
with the many Conyers' quarterings, that
stood beside the lighted waxen taper ready
for service, but not at the boy. When he
did look up, there was the bright, sunny
smile that he had learned to love so well,
and the clear blue eyes met his as pleasantly
as if their owner had never yet known care
or sorrow.

Darrell's short letter, then, was promptly written and despatched, under convoy of his grandfather's more pretentious epistle. It contained nothing that was in any way inappropriate, when addressed by a lad to his old teacher. There was merely the expression of an earnest hope that the tutor would consent to accept a secure competence at Sir Peregrine's hands. And then the boy added, that he asked Mr. Meanwell to agree to the proposal as an especial and personal favour to himself, and so oblige, " ever sincerely yours, Darrell Conyers."

And so the two letters were forwarded, Sir Peregrine never suspecting that their relative weight with the recipient might be in an inverse ratio to the length and verbosity of the contents, or to the standing of those who had penned them.

Diplomatists who have got beyond the rudiments of their profession, chuckle as they tell how, along with some fulminant despatch, some portentous protocol, bruited by the journals as likely to set all Europe

by the ears, there travels meekly in a corner
of the crimson leather bag borne by a state
messenger, a short, straightforward note, not
worded in the circumlocutory jargon meant
to be printed in blue books, yellow books,
red books, yet which serves in half an hour
to conjure away the war-cloud looming so
threateningly on the political horizon.

It was not until a later day that Sir Peregrine could divine which had told the most
with the humble north-country tutor—his
own tempting offer, urbanely couched as to
terms, or the curt, irresistible summons of
Darrell Conyers. It is perhaps as well that
we do not always analyze the motives of
those who serve our purpose.

CHAPTER XIV.

ON THE BRIDGE.

THERE were at Crag Towers more terraces than one. There was the Green Terrace overlooking the dry moat, the Stone Terrace, gay with scarlet geraniums in their season, and decked with marble statuary, in the grand garden that had been laid out when Europe danced to the piping of Versailles; and there was the Water Terrace, perhaps the least frequented of the three. This last was flagged with coarse, gray-blue marble from a once famous quarry of the Welsh Marches, a material which had been used for the effigy of many a cross-legged templar, and many a wimpled dame, stretched on a mediæval tombstone in some local chancel, but which was neglected now that the

sculptor could draw his supplies from the
rocky hill-sides of southern Europe. It
had been built between the mansion and
the river that laved it, when the peaceful
lapse of time had made it clear that the
indwellers were no longer to be startled
from their slumbers by the war-cry of the
wild Welsh, and that it would not .be
a suicidal proceeding to give a foeman
standing-room between the Castle wall and
the fast-flowing river. As it was, the
broad, flat stones actually projected over
the stream beneath; while at one extremity,
where rock and wall came down sheer to
the Wye, there was barely room for the
passage of a human being bent on reaching
the wider space beyond.

This so-called Water Terrace was a favourite resort of Miss Conyers, a preference for
which there may perhaps have been more
reasons than one. It was quiet and solitary,
skirting. as it did that older part of the
Castle of which many rooms were un-
occupied. Then, too, it afforded whoever

traversed it a pretty prospect of the rocks
and the river; and a good, though over-
near view of the picturesquely castellated
pile that towered grimly overhead. And
Adeline was keenly alive to the associations
that clung to the scarred wall and the
mouldering turrets beneath which she
sometimes loved to linger; for did not
these feudal surroundings tell of the old
times when the strong hand bore sway,
and the modern doctrines of which the
preachers are as legion were but as yet
in the egg! At any rate the place was
one which suited well with her taste, and
Darrell, one lowering morning, when the
dark clouds came sailing by, and the
swallows dipped their rapid wings in the
water as they darted after the flies, would
not have been surprised to see her there,
as he softly opened the window of his room
in the west wing, had it not been that she
was not alone. Miss Conyers was standing
on the edge of the stony platform, in an
attitude of calm and cold reserve, while

before her stood another female form, a
shapeless bundle of clothes, so to speak,
topped by a structure of tulle and ribbons
that simulated a bonnet; neatly gloved,
neatly booted; but crouching against the
wall with gesticulations that implied a
lively terror of toppling over from the edge
of the steep terrace, which was guarded
by no rail or parapet, into the eddying river
below.

" What have we here? " Such was the
boy's first reflection. " Not a beggar,
surely; or a mad woman? A lady smuggler,
rather, who desires to talk my accomplished
kinswoman into buying her trashy shawls,
worthless silks, and sham jewellery, at fancy
prices. A shrewd old beldam she looks,"
he added, as he caught sight of the
swarthy, bony visage, the cunning eyes,
and the expressive mouth of Madame
Veuve Tracrenard. " A foreigner, of course,
and not likely, by her appearance, to get
the worst of a bargain. Well, let her cheat
my loving relative, if she be so minded !

I do not find the part of eavesdropper so much to my taste that I care to play it without a stake on the game." And he was about to withdraw, when suddenly his falcon eye lit on the face of Adeline, which had hitherto been averted, and the expression of which at once riveted his attention. "This, I suspect, has more of the flavour of tragedy about it than I imagined it to have," he murmured softly; and as he spoke he drew back his head to avoid the risk of detection, should Miss Conyers chance to look up; and, screened by the thick-growing ivy, kept a vigilant watch on those below. Very pale, careworn, and eager was Adeline's beautiful face, as she turned it towards the widow.

"You have broken faith with me! You have been false to your word, or you would not be here!" said Adeline, speaking rapidly, and in the French language; but the words were not lost on the young listener above.

Then Madame Tracrenard spread out her

gloved hands with a deprecatory gesture,
and said, or mumbled, something which
Adeline, in her quick, imperious way,
promptly interrupted.

"*Trève d'excuses!*" said Miss Conyers,
in her clear, incisive accents. "You reason
like Molière's Sgaranelle, but you waste
your breath in the useless labour. Enough
that where there is the carrion of a secret,
the birds of prey will gather to rend and
tear and flesh their foul beaks, and preen
their noisome wings above the prize. I
might have known that so long as there
was a problematic five-franc piece to be
extracted from my hopes or my fears, your
vulture instinct would not be sated. What!
you came to render me a service, you say?
How fortunate I am in the possession of so
considerate a friend! Yet this is no fit
place for the reception of your disinterested
confidence."

The Frenchwoman's reply was inaudible,
but Adeline's next words came with perfect
distinctness to the listener's ears, accom-

panied as they were by a scornful gesture
of her slender arm and hand.

"Why do you cower and grovel yonder,
like a toad or a lizard that squeezes itself
against a rock in the hope to avoid being
seen and slain? Are you seized with a
sudden giddiness; or do you verily suspect
that I am likely to succumb to temptation,
and thrust you over, and watch you drown,
in the river that washes these old stones?
Reassure yourself, chère Madame Tracrenard. Were there no other obstacles to so
simple a method of severing our connection,
I am not capable of such an action. It
would be worse than a crime, for it would
be a blunder, too, as a wit of your own
nation, of whom you have probably never
heard, won renown by declaring. You are
quite safe beside me."

Thus adjured, although with awkward
unwillingness, Veuve Tracrenard ventured
to crawl to Adeline's side; and a few words
were then exchanged, but in too low a tone
to be overheard at the window above. At

the moment of parting, however, the
sound of the Frenchwoman's voice reached
Darrell.

"At three o'clock, then," she said, in
slightly louder accents than those which
she had previously employed, "and this
very day, I shall expect you. Three, then,
and without fail ! "

" Without fail ! " repeated Miss Conyers,
half mechanically, as it seemed.

" *Jusqu'alors, mademoiselle?* " said the
Widow Tracrenard, in a tone of affected
humility; and she shuffled off, keeping as
close as possible to the wall to which she
clung, and uttering a groan or an ejacula-
tion each time that her eye fell on the
seething water that leaped and bubbled so
near. Adeline stood motionless until the
last flutter of Madame Tracrenard's dress
was lost to sight, and then, with a wild
rapidity quite unlike her usual stately
grace, clasped her two hands together and
uplifted them as if in prayer, at the same
time raising her face towards heaven, while

her lips moved, but no sound passed them. Then she allowed her arms to drop, heavy and helpless, beside her, and slowly shrank away. One glance, and only one, had Darrell time to obtain of her white, desperate face, and then she was gone, with bent-down head and hasty tread, swiftly skirting the walls, and soon disappearing from sight.

"So, so, my good kinswoman," muttered Darrell, as with his eyes he followed the retiring figure, "you have your little mysteries, it appears, for all your disdainful dignity of bearing. What I have witnessed a moment since confirms what I imagined weeks ago, with regard to the secret errand on which you had been bound on that early morning when the careless slamming of my door startled us both as I watched you. '*Trois heures, sans faute!*' It is well that I have not forgotten my French. The appointment holds for three this day, then, although I did not hear where the tryst was to be kept. Wherever the meeting may

take place it will be my own fault if there
are not three, instead of two, present at the
interview."

To watch another person well and closely,
yet without affording to the object of this
vigilance any warning indication that his
or her actions are being chronicled, is of
itself an art; and in this art women excel.
Their patience, their intuitive powers of
divining motives, and the almost micro-
scopic ability for noting trifles which belongs
to the sex, qualifies most of Eve's daughters
to surpass, in this, their own line, the skill
of a Vidocq. It is true that when you set
a woman to watch a woman, Greek is pitted
against Greek, and the tug of war begins.
If the spy can tread on velvet feet, and see
without looking, these immemorial feminine
privileges are no enigmas to the adversary,
whose fine perceptions enable her to feel,
rather than to learn by any of the coarse
processes of masculine logic, that unfriendly
eyes are upon her. Then follows a contest
of social finessing, a species of airy *kriegspiel*

ON THE BRIDGE.   285

limited by no rules, and in which the moves
are too slight and subtle to be narrated in
plain words. That Darrell was no friend of
hers Miss Conyers well knew; but even she,
whom it behoved for certain reasons to be
ever on her guard, and who looked with a
jealous anxiety at all faces where she might
read the possible traces of suspicion, little
dreamed that Darrell saw, and was amused
to see, the successful efforts which she made
to play her part well before the world.
There was nothing about this bright boy
to suggest that feline method of scrutinizing
every movement of the chosen object which
we naturally identify with the practices of
the domestic detective. He went out and
came in as it was habitual for him to do,
and did not address a dozen words to Adeline
Conyers during the entire morning.

Luncheon in a country house, an important meal with women, is apt to be
neglected or forgotten by the rougher sex.
But the small family party at Crag Towers
assembled with commendable regularity

around the hospitable board, Sir Peregrine
being too old, his grandson too young, and
Craven too glad to find himself in Nellie's
society, to permit of that midday separation
between the two sections of the household
above-stairs, to which modern custom lends
its sanction. The weather had justified its
proverbial renown for fickleness, since the
threatening rain-clouds had rolled away and
a hot and oppressive day had succeeded to
the menace of the morning. There was
some outstanding pledge that the two
sisters, with their cousin the captain,
should cross the park to the commodore's
cottage. That encyclopædic nutshell was
on that day to be enriched by a new attrac-
tion—it mattered little what—perhaps some
new flower, monster strawberry, or preposterous melon of Scipio's raising, or a fresh
mechanical puzzle or labour-saving contri-
vance, sprung from the brain of the negro's
inventive master, claimed half an hour's
attention. But Adeline, who had shown no
signs of any mental pre-occupation, simply

asked of the others to make her excuses to
worthy Captain Killick and Grace his niece.
The heat, she said, of the sultry day was
greater than she would willingly encounter.
Then Sir Peregrine, who had his own appointment at the home farm, went off to
hear his knowing bailiff discuss the points
of shorthorned cattle and the merits of
oilcake; and grateful Nellie, who believed
her sister to be thoughtfully desirous to
secure her a pleasant stroll across the turf
in Craven's company, came up and kissed
her warmly. The caress was not returned,
but presently Craven and Nellie were gone,
and Darrell had strolled off with his fishing
rod, and Miss Conyers was left alone.

On that side of the park which is farthest
from Gridley Green and from the commodore's cottage, there gurgles, flows, and
trickles, according to the amount of the
rainfall, a little stream which bears locally
the name of the Kightle. That brook must
have run crimson-red on one day at least
within the historical period, for its shallow

waters wash the base of the Welshmen's
Hill, where stood the camp of the Britons
who last begirt the Norman stronghold of
Crag Towers, and who left behind them many
a corpse, and many a wounded warrior to
be speared by the English men-at-arms or
brained by the enraged peasantry, when the
pennon and the lances of Conyers broke
through their white-mantled phalanx. The
stream is spanned by a narrow foot bridge of
massive timber, almost old enough for its
weather-stained planks to have creaked
beneath the hurrying feet of the flying
Welsh, and a high stile in the tall deer
paling gives access to a little path which
leads directly to this foot-bridge. Few are
those, however, who traverse that rarely
trodden track, which is called by the villagers the Keeper's Road. That angle of
the park is a marshy one, where rushes
and heather and coarse herbage and dock
leaves usurp the place of the feathery fern
and crisp venison grass, and where the black
earth is retentive of water. There is one

clump of trees, the silvery stems of the birch mingling with the dark bolls of the alder, which stands at easy pistol range from the nearer end of the bridge.

Adeline Conyers, as she stole from the mansion of her fathers towards the Kightle and the bridge, towards three o'clock on the afternoon of the day on which she had promised to have a second interview with the Frenchwoman, was but too conscious of the humiliation which her errand involved. The descendant of old conquerors was bound for a trysting-place whence she dared not to absent herself, beneath the shadow of the very hill which had witnessed the triumph of her martial ancestor. Here, where her ruthless race had governed the Marches with ample powers and stern sway, she was compelled to elude unwelcome notice as best she might, and to scheme, and feign, and bide her time, that no tattling tongues might be busy with her name. As she went she lifted her head, now and again casting furtive glances to left and right, as if to assure herself that her course was not tracked by any inquisitive observer. The park was strictly kept, in theory at least, for the private recreation of the family at the Castle. There was not even a legal right of way for pedestrians using the grass-grown path. But all human enactments have a tendency to relax themselves, and accordingly rustic urchins would sometimes gather mushrooms on the uplands, or old women collect dry sticks among the glades, unreproved. There were no such gleaners visible as Miss Conyers advanced to the swampy meadow that bordered on the stream, and saw that she was the first to keep the appointment. Veuve Tracrenard had not as yet arrived.

Adeline, as she passed the thick-growing clump of trees of which mention has been made, fancied that she heard the snapping of a rotten twig beneath some careless tread; but though she halted for a while, as her restless eyes narrowly scanned the thicket,

she saw and heard nothing more. The
wooden bridge once reached, she leaned
against one of the sturdy handrails, the
paint on which was peeled and blistered
by sun and rain, and gazed with vacant eyes
at the thread of water that babbled around
the great smooth stones, beneath which, in
tiny pools, lay small fish—the bearded loach,
the silvery minnow, the quaint bullhead,
each to himself the centre of his cramped
world, as vain man is of his, and eagerly
engrossed with the twin instincts of prey
and self-preservation. The brook had
shrunk to a fourth of its ordinary winter
width, and contained many a shoal of
smooth pebbles and bar of rough gravel;
while in one place a knot of willow trees
overhung the bank, serving as a support for
a tangled screen of broom, bramble, and
wild honeysuckle, that clung to wrinkled
stem and bare rock impartially. This
coppice was some few paces, six or seven
perhaps, from the bridge; and Adeline, whose
face had been turned from it, started, as a

bird, apparently scared from its nest, flew
forth from the boughs with a scream. But
in the next instant she saw the Frenchwoman, who had slowly scaled the stile,
approaching her.

Darrell's promise to himself that there
should be a third person present at his
kinswoman's interview with the foreigner
had been no idle vaunt. He had reckoned,
almost to a minute, the precise time
when Miss Conyers would be likely to leave
the house, and had formed a shrewd guess
that her probable route would lead her
across some portion of the park, at that
hour by far the most solitary part of the
demesne. But he had had need of all his
activity, speed, and readiness of resource,
to follow unperceived, when first, from his
chosen post among some rook-haunted elms,
he marked the line that Adeline seemed to
take. The broken ground favoured him in
some degree, while the skill with which he
availed himself of every patch of fern,
every hollow, bank, or tree, creeping at one

time, running swiftly at another, when some
friendly bushes or swelling hillock screened
him from view, and later still, couching
himself amidst moss and heather when the
object of his pursuit showed indications of
turning to look back, would have done
credit to the wiliest bush-fighter that ever
practised against a savage enemy the stratagems of the wilderness. Nor could the
Indian on the war-path, prowling for scalps
and plunder around a settlement of the
hated whites, have glided more adroitly
into a lurking-place than did Darrell when
he slid silently down the bank of the brook,
and took refuge in the midst of the osiers
and fantastic willow roots that projected
from the crumbling soil, screened from
observation by the undergrowth and matted
brambles.

From this his chosen place of espial the
boy was an unseen witness of the meeting
between Miss Conyers and Veuve Tracrenard. In one respect his ambush was in-
efficient, since, strain his ears as he might,

to catch the slightest sound of a spoken
word, he could hear nothing. The conversation, although evidently energetic, and at
times impassioned, was still cautiously carried on, and the voices of the speakers only
reached Darrell as an indistinct murmur.
But among our mercurial neighbours the
science of gesticulation has been pushed
to such perfection that it is often possible
to divine the spirit of a dialogue by means
of the eyes alone. Thus it was plain that
at the first Madame Tracrenard, with out-
spread hands, and bent body, and upturned
face, was deferentially deprecating the re-
proaches that fell fast from Adeline's lips.
Presently it seemed her turn to speak; long,
glibly, purringly, as a cat endowed with
human speech might be supposed to do.
Anon, she was shaking her head doggedly
but humbly, and obviously holding out,
with passive stubbornness, against the fiery
eagerness with which Adeline pressed some
argument.

" Easy to see who wins ! " Such was the

boy's mute comment as he watched the debate; and scarcely had the unuttered thought passed through his mind before he saw Adeline place some object in the Frenchwoman's ready hand, at the same time receiving, as in exchange, another. Veuve Tracrenard coolly opened the crimson leather *écrin* which she held, and drew forth from it something sparkling, something that flashed as the sun's rays fell upon its brightness. A diamond necklace, surely, and by the glint and glitter, one of no trifling value. What Adeline had received was simply a book bound in dark purple, and fastened by a gilt clasp. Few were the words that were said, after this barter had been effected; and with a cold and scant leave-taking the late associates separated, the foreigner making the best of her way out of the park, while Miss Conyers, without once looking back, returned to the house, carrying her book concealed beneath the light scarf that she wore. She reached the mansion, the west wing, and her room, without any inconvenient encounter, and had hardly closed her door before Darrell, flushed and panting, gained the broad oaken landing-place that she had left behind her.

"Fairly run to earth!" Such was his breathless soliloquy. "And now I can follow no farther. Will she burn it? I think not. People, and ladies above all people, seldom care to burn what they have bought at such a price. A book! Had it been a packet of letters, now, I could have guessed the purport of the costly purchase. But a book! It must be curious reading, that volume!" And with a strange smile he turned away.

CHAPTER XV.

THE BRASS KEY.

ONCE safely in her room, a great and sudden change came over the ordinarily haughty and impassive Adeline. She had borne herself, during the trying interview with Widow Tracrenard, with a dignity and a courage that had remained unshaken even by the vehemence of her emotion. But once at home, in her chamber, and beyond the reach of prying eyes, her pride melted as the Alpine snows thaw before the warm breath of the " Fohn " wind, and the tears fell in blinding showers from those cold eyes that to outward observers had seemed proof against any sign of feminine weakness. Miss Conyers was not one of those who weep easily. It required no slight

shock to stir in her the storm of mingled
rage and anguish that broke through all the
barriers of icy self-restraint. But the tempest of conflicting passions was now fairly
aroused, and would have its course. Adeline threw herself, wildly sobbing, on the
bed, and hid her tear-stained face among
the yielding pillows, as some love-lorn
damsel in her teens might have done.
Where, now, was the curb of her long
training in that worldly school that looks
on sorrow as a solecism, and despair as a
subject fit for the stage alone—the academy
of those drawing-room Stoics who politely
ignore the darker side both of human life
and of human nature? Of such philosophy
Sir Peregrine's eldest daughter had been
reckoned a promising pupil. But she felt
too strongly, too fiercely, always to be able
to maintain in private the smooth serenity
that duped the world without.

The necessity for action roused her from
her first paroxysm of wounded pride, and
wrath, and shame. Dashing away the hot

tears, she rose, and proceeded with thoughtful care to efface from her wet cheek and
dimmed eyes the traces of her recent emotion, smoothing back, too, her loosened
hair, and adjusting her disordered dress.
Then she drew forth the book that she had
received from Veuve Tracrenard's hand,
and which, as if by instinct, she had till
then concealed beneath the pillow on which
her head had rested. A thin octavo volume,
bound, as has been said, in purple cloth,
the colour of which years had slightly
faded, and fastened with a gilded clasp, it
presented as to its outward aspect nothing
in the least remarkable. Yet Adeline, as
she stood, holding the book between her
jewelled fingers, looked on it with somewhat
of the stony horror with which we can
imagine the dilating eyes of Cleopatra to
have fixed themselves on the asp, which,
with its lithe folds and venomed fang,
afforded a last sad refuge from Roman ven-
geance to the conquered daughter of the
Ptolemies. Almost mechanically, her gaze

ranged around the room. It was hot summer weather, and as a natural consequence the large low grate, with its bright bars and fender of burnished steel, was cold and empty. A taper, however, stood among the writing materials on a little table of red-mottled marble, and this Adeline lighted. She had but to open the book, to apply fire to the edges of the rustling leaves, and to let the blazing volume drop upon the hearth beside her, sure that the heap of blackened tinder and charred boards would tell no tales. Yet she hesitated.

It is fortunate, no doubt, for the cause of civilization, that so many and various documents, which it was distinctly against the interest of writers or keepers to preserve, have escaped the flames. Hundreds of men and women have built, as it were, a high pillory whereon their shades should do perpetual penance, by the free use of pen and ink. We should think well of, or indulgently forget, many and many a personage of ancient or modern times, were it not

for the hoarded correspondence that has
made him or her for ever notorious. And,
oddly enough, it has often, and for a series
of years, been in the power of these self-
branded outlaws of the moral code to
destroy every scrap of the recorded evi-
dence against them. This statesman might
have veiled his treason, yonder prince concealed his breach of faith, the great lady
not have given the lie to the fulsome praise
on her gorgeous tombstone, the patriot
have hushed the jingle of bribes in his
pocket, the braggart of honesty not have
registered himself a rogue in grain.

Miss Conyers, holding the book within
a few inches of the lighted taper, did not
burn it. Why, or from the influence of
what complex chain of motives, the subtlest
analyst of the heart would have been puzzled to say. But certain it is, that after
some minutes of thought she extinguished
the light, laying the book carefully on the
table near her, and then, seating herself
near the open window, she leaned her head

upon her arm, and pondered long and deeply. Then she rose, and, carrying the book, as before, hidden among the folds of her scarf, she left the room. The precaution which she had taken was, it seemed, superfluous. Between her own chamber and the picture gallery she encountered no one. She entered the gallery, and traversed it slowly and with a strange but manifest reluctance, drooping her head and lowering her eyes, as if to avoid the cold stare of the many portraits that watched her as she went. They were but painted canvas after all, those effigies of the dead: durable shadows, signed by the initials of names once famous, and some few of which had not yet lost the charm that clings to the productions of Vandyke, Holbein, and Lely. Yet, as Adeline passed between the lines of pictures, she felt as if arraigned for trial and judgment before a ghostly tribunal chosen from the ancient stock from which she sprang. She could have fancied that the hollow suits of armour, placed at

intervals beside the walls, stirred and rattled as she passed, and that the nodding
casque and tall crest of each mail-clad
presentment of a knight assumed a threatening air as her tread awoke the echoes.
At the end of the gallery was a species of
cabinet in carved oak, let into the wall—
the handiwork, to judge by the bold yet
elaborate style, of some clever pupil of
Gibbons. There were wyverns, and scaly
dragons, and salamanders, and the figures
of armed men, standing forth from the
brown surface of the old oak; and a large
lock of quaint construction, such as we
may occasionally meet with in some Flem-
ish castle or convent; a relic of the days
when the painstaking artisans of Ghent or
Ypres set lessons to the world. This cabinet was now never used or opened. Adeline
could remember that when she was a child
its shelves had supported sundry queer old
pieces of massive plate, hanaps of silver,
parcel-gilt goblets, and peg-tankards wherein
had simmered and frothed the nut-brown

ale and the dark metheglin of simpler generations. But, for years past, the cabinet had contained nothing but cracked monstrosities in Dutch ceramic ware or chipped china; and as Adeline turned the heavy brass key, the lock groaned complainingly, and with a sullen sound the unwilling hinges turned on their rusty pivots. For one moment she paused, as if wavering in her purpose; but in the next, and almost violently, she flung the purple-bound book deep into the cupboard, and, locking the door, withdrew the key, and hurried from the spot. Not a glance did she throw at the pictured faces on the walls, but swept from the gallery with the quickened step and resentful mien of one who quits an hostile assembly.

It is hard to bear about the burthen of a secret, and to preserve before indifferent or curious eyes an aspect of serene equanimity. Yet such is the lot of not a few men, and of many women. Poor Crœsus, bank director, chairman of boards auriferous,

member of unimpeachable clubs, fellow of
Royal Societies, a parliament man, a family
man, above all things a man of money,
deserves pity now and then as he blandly
swaggers forward, with florid face and trim
whiskers, rattling the heavy gold chain that
crosses his goodly white waistcoat. He
dares not flinch. Too many friends, foes,
dependants, watch him, for it to be safe for
one so eminent to seem careworn or unhappy. A sigh would be equivalent to a
confession. Hang-dog looks would occasion
a run upon the bank. Credit would col-
lapse like a soap-bubble were it suspected
that the golden image had feet of clay.
Wherefore, and in hopes of better times,
our man of money tides on as best he may,
well knowing that the coin of which he
is composed is but base and spurious, certain to be nailed with ignominy to the
counter, if once its cracked ring or dull
jingle be detected by the ears of experts.

Adeline showed no particular signs of
mental preoccupation on that day, whether

during the remainder of the sunny hours,
or at dinner. That her head ached, and
that the heat of the weather was distaste-
ful to her, she frankly admitted. But she
talked gently and graciously, and was, perhaps, a more entertaining member of the
company than it was her wont to be. Sir
Peregrine, too, was in an unusually affable
mood. Various circumstances had combined to sweeten the baronet's temper.
The dispute between himself and his accom-.
plished elder daughter had been comfortably
arranged. He was to keep Darrell at home
with him at Crag Towers, and yet with
such provision for the boy's education as
would prevent self-constituted censors from
charging him with preferring his own senile
affection for his grandson to the well-being
of the youthful heir. He was able to do
what in homely parlance is styled "a good
turn" to Mr. Meanwell, without running
the risk of being made ridiculous by the
probable blunders and rustic awkwardness
of that exemplary tutor, as an inmate of

the Castle. Then, too, a farm, let by Sir
Peregrine's father for a lease of lives, had,
as the steward phrased it, "fallen in"—a
result bringing with it a certain addition
of at least a thousand pounds a year to the
Conyers' rent-roll, besides the satisfaction
of ensuring that dilapidated buildings, barbarous husbandry, and ill-drained fields,
should no longer make an eyesore of a
valuable portion of the property.

Sir Peregrine, therefore, instead of pur-
suing his usual habits, chose to doze away
the warm evening in the drawing-room,
and more than once, on awaking from a
short siesta, made inquiry for Adeline, to
whose fine voice he was partial, and whom
he wished to sing to him, as she sometimes, though rarely, did. But Adeline
was absent. She had glided, unperceived
even by Darrell, from the house, and
through the dusk and shadows of evening
had made her way across the park. She
walked fast—very fast, availing herself of
the friendly gloom which the leafy glades

cast upon the turf, and diverging often
from the direct path rather than cross
some broad expanse of open ground where
her form would be too distinctly visible.
Of whose questioning, or of whose vigilance
she was afraid, she scarcely knew. She
was aware, however, that the world at large
is Argus-eyed where the peccadilloes of a
social superior are in question, and that the
lightest whisper concerning herself would
circulate through the village with the
rapidity of wildfire, should some untoward
accident betray her to any hanger-on of
the mansion.

Of being at home before her absence
should excite suspicion or inquiry, Miss
Conyers had little doubt. Nellie and Craven would be too intent on each other's
society to note her disappearance. Darrell
would probably have strayed off in search
of some amusement befitting his age. Sir
Peregrine would be among his books and
letters. No one, were she but speedy,
would realize the length of her stay abroad,

or even conjecture the nature of her occupation. So she reasoned, pushing on the while, until she reached the spot which she had selected. Then, kneeling, she drew forth the massive brass key of the oaken cabinet, and buried it, beneath moist earth and crumbling stone, beneath rank grass and interlacing bramble, in a nook solitary and neglected enough, so it seemed, to keep the hidden thing confided to it until the Last Day. It was done. Breathless, flushed, and eager, she arose from her knees, and slowly quitted the hollow among the bushes, and emerged into the pure light of the newly-risen moon. Then she saw, and started to see, that her dainty hands were besmeared with the marks of wet clay, and that there were green stains from the dewy grass, and miry stains from the moist mould, on the light summer dress that she wore. Hastily she dipped her fingers in the water of the brook, and then hurried home with the speed of a hunted animal.

By this time the truant had been missed.

It is one of the privileges which wealth and
rank confer upon a woman that she should
have abundant elbow-room and large leisure
—should be free, in fact, from the petty if
wholesome restraints which beset ladies of
limited income. Men, poor or rich, are so
free as to their outgoings and incomings,
that they hardly realize the amount of
supervision under which their wives, sisters,
and mothers pass what are very probably
lives as blameless and excellent as any
chronicled by hagiologists. There is somewhat of claustral discipline in the practice
of those households where every female's
time has to be accounted for by measured
minutes : where the sheep are perpetually
counted by amateur shepherds ; and where
an absence of a quarter of an hour is written
down in the books of the recording seraph.
Miss Conyers was in general mistress of her
actions. But Sir Peregrine's presence, and
his whim that his eldest daughter should
sing to him, made this evening exceptional,
and led to the fact that when Adeline came

in, Darrell was lounging in the great entrance hall, among the stags' heads, and
the cumbrous marbles, and the fluted pillars
that some Conyers virtuoso had brought
from a ruinous palace and ruined *principe*
in Ravenna or Milan. He said nothing, and
did not, to all appearance, give a second
thought to the defaulter's appearance; yet
there was not a stain on her dress, not a
disordered tress of her flaxen hair, not a
gesture, that he did not note; and this
she more than guessed as she hurried by.

So quick were Adeline's movements, that
every misadventure to her toilet was re-
paired, and no tell-tale marks of the errand
on which she had been engaged remained
to testify against her, when Nellie at
length came to ask if she were ill, and to
mention that their father had repeatedly
inquired for her. Five minutes more, and
Miss Conyers was seated at the piano in
the great cool drawing-room. She sang
sweetly and skilfully, with a world of
power and of tender expression welling up

in the clear notes of her admirably modulated voice. Her headache, she said, was
nearly gone. She had walked for a few
minutes in the gardens, and had been
reposing also upstairs. The rest and the
fresh air had acted as talismans. She
would sing again, if her father pleased, a
certain old ballad that had been a favourite
with him always. And this she did sing,
much to Sir Peregrine's contentment, while
Darrell, with a half smile playing about his
well-shaped mouth, leaned against the massive mantelpiece, listening to the music of
that rich, ringing voice.

Late on that night, when all in the Castle
were in bed, and presumably asleep, and the
moonlight streamed like molten silver on
the grim stones of the grey old Norman
keep, it poured like a flood of shimmering
radiance between the open curtains of
Darrell's chamber. The boy was awake
still. The moon, the rays of which, pale,
cold, and pure, seemed to caress his cheek,
had ridden high in the heavens, and was

stooping now towards the setting-place of both sun and moon. That pearly lustre lit up, in all the range of its travels, no fairer face as to features, none nobler or more candid as to expression, than that of Sir Peregrine's heir. Seen thus, the beautiful boy might have been an angel, watching while others slumbered, for the good of erring man. He sat in the window, the sash of which was raised, to permit the light breeze to play around his temples, as, with his head resting on his arm, he gazed thoughtfully down to where, at the bottom of rock and wall, a sheer descent of many feet, the river ran. There he sat, musing more intently and more patiently than seemed natural to one so young, and before whom so smiling a prospect in the great panorama of life lay full of joyous promise.

A strange contrast. There, below, ran the brattling Wye, a true Cymric river, that seemed to have much of the impetuous character of the western British race whose birthplace was, like its own parent fountain, among the crags and glens of the bleak and barren principality. It seethed and boiled below, fretting around the water-worn stones against which it had waged war for many a year and many an age before the eagle standards, and the tall helmets, and the glittering shields, came down to be mirrored in the pellucid streams as Ostorius Scapula and his legionaries crossed in pursuit of Caradoc. And there was the boy, one day to be lord of the fortress-mansion, suddenly called from poverty to take his seat among the fortunate of the earth, keeping vigil thus, in calm thoughtfulness, while every other eye was closed, every other brain at rest. At last, with a kindled flash of exultation in his blue eyes, he sprang from his seat. "I have it!" he exclaimed, with a soft low laugh of inward triumph. "Yes, at last I have it! I hold the end of the clue, and to-morrow—yes, to-morrow—I'll track it out to the end of the skein." And he closed the window with a brisk slam, and laughed again, with an air of quiet enjoyment, as he turned away.

Soon after this Darrell was asleep, a stray gleam of moonlight touching the golden curls of the young head that lay so peacefully on the pillow. The lips were slightly parted, the graceful head resting on one arm, in a careless attitude of repose; and there was a smile on the sleeper's face—an innocent, happy smile, such as we associate with the idea of guileless youth spent in the midst of genial prosperity and tender care. The moon slowly sank, and white mists, like warning phantoms that fleeted past, hovered along the silent Wye, where now, save for the river's murmur, every sound was hushed, and in grange and farmhouse, in hall and hovel, all were locked in that slumber which, like the longer sleep that it simulates, is common to us all.

END OF VOL. I.